M000207287

BEST MICROFICTION

2021

Series Editors

Meg Pokrass, Gary Fincke

Guest Editor

Amber Sparks

BEST MICROFICTION 2021
ISBN: 978-1-949790-44-3
eISBN: 978-1-949790-45-0

Copyright © 2021 Best Microfiction. All material used
by permission with rights retained by the original copyright holder.

First Pelekinesis Printing 2021

For information:

Pelekinesis
112 Harvard Ave #65
Claremont, CA 91711 USA

ISSN 2641-9750

www.pelekinesis.com

Best
Microfiction
2021

Best Microfiction Anthology Series

Series Editors
Meg Pokrass, Gary Fincke

Guest Editor
Amber Sparks

Contributing Editor, North America
Bill Cook

Contributing Editor, Australasia
Rachel Smith

Special Features/Contributing Editor
Pat Foran

Contributing Editors
Clare Weze, Frances Gapper, Dan Crawley,
Exodus Octavia Brownlow, Jonathan Cardew

Production Editor
Cooper Renner

Social Media Manager
T. Guzman

Copy Editor
Michelle Christophorou

Layout and Design
Mark Givens

Cover illustration
Terry M. Givens

TABLE OF CONTENTS

TWO ESSAYS ON CRAFT

WHAT THE EDITORS SAY: INTERVIEWS WITH THE YEAR'S TOP MICROFICTION MAGAZINES

FOREWORD

MEG POKRASS AND GARY FINCKE,
SERIES CO-EDITORS

Best Microfiction is now three years old and rapidly
growing into the diverse, international anthology
series we envisioned at the outset. It's been a joy
to read the submissions of editors from literary
journals from many continents Likewise, it's been
wonderful working with our first three guest editors,
Dan Chaon, Michael Martone, and Amber Sparks,
all of whom have chosen a full spectrum of voices,
forms, and aesthetics across the nearly 100 stories
selected annually.

It's a good time to reflect on how the *Best Microfiction* series has evolved. Happily established, our
anthology demonstrates that we're growing and
changing rather than leaning toward a particular type
of writing or a selection based on precedent. Now
in our third volume, we have evolved into a yearly
anthology with a focus on selections from small,
online lit journals. These magazines are labors of
love, and we celebrate all of their quirky brilliance.

Every year our guest editor has the opportunity
to create an eclectic selection enriched with their

personal sense of what resonates and makes them excited about the possibilities of the form. Here, readers will see that *Best Microfiction*'s 2021 Guest Editor, Amber Sparks, has chosen original, risk-taking, unclassifiable gems.

INTRODUCTION

AMBER SPARKS, GUEST EDITOR

"An unfinished story." "A sketch." "A vignette." These are the phrases the writer of very short stories and essays often encounters, as if the artistry of creative writing were determined entirely by length. As if the short form were not an electric, exciting, energizing form entirely its own, borrowing little from the long form but the use of words lined up in a row. As if these writers were anything but precise, intentional, breathtaking in their word choice and placement.

In reading these submissions, I was struck by the diversity of structures and subjects, by the wild experimentation, by the sheer freedom the form seemed to give these writers. There seemed at times a hurricane blowing through these pieces, a sort of urgency you only find in writers in the midst of pleasure in pushing the envelope.

I truly believe that these are the writers to watch in the contemporary lit scene; they are inventing something entirely new, and whether or not the critics catch up probably doesn't matter much to them. This is writing at its most daring, its most alive, and I feel lucky and honored to have been able to witness the future unfolding. All the writers I read were frankly fantastic, but the stories here often have that something extra, that ineffable quality that may be called inspiration, I suppose. Or maybe just bravery? I clapped, I shouted, I howled while reading some of these, so daring and so new they felt. I hope they strike you that way, too, and that you enjoy reading them as much as I did.

BEST MICROFICTION

SISTERS

CEZARIJA ABARTIS

No, it's not my fault, now Mama will punish me
and I didn't mean to do it and neighbors will think
I'm a bad girl and no it was an accident and I'm
innocent and it wasn't like I killed anybody, I didn't
mean to break the bowl and I'll save my allowance
and buy another one, but no, Mama will say it was
her grandma's and there's no replacement of such
a treasure because her grandma died and is in the
cold dark ground from which there is no escape, no
salvation, no joy and all we have is what we have
above ground under the sun and moon and I once
said that the gravestone is under the sun too but she
looked at me as if I was crazy-insane and told me
to go take a nap in my room and turn off the light
and see if I wanted to talk back to her anymore but
I wasn't talking back and Mama paced on the carpet
up and down and then she telephoned Daddy and
said her uncle in Ireland had died and she hadn't
seen him since she was a child so why was she upset
I wondered, lots of people have died, and of course
we all will die and be put in the ground—I know

that and nobody gets out alive Daddy says—but all I did today was brush up against the bowl and maybe it's true I was mad at my sister and maybe I flicked my arm at her but she had called me a stinkybreath who would never find anyone to love me, nobody never, and my arm lashed out and pushed the bowl off the mantel and it didn't even touch Molly, who laughed at me and said now I was in real trouble and she would go tell Mama who would for sure ground me for a month and I hate my sister and hope she dies the death and I know Mama will forgive me and I will collect up the broken pieces and put them on a newspaper so she can see I'm sorry and yes I love her and Daddy but not Molly who I will forever hate, well maybe not forever, and yes, maybe I'll forgive her, I am a saint, I am a good girl, yes, I know she's an ignorant foolish person, yes, and I'll forgive her, yes.

Cezarija Abartis has published a collection, *Nice Girls and Other Stories* (New Rivers Press) and stories in *Bennington Review*, *Columbia Journal*, *FRiGG*, *matchbook*, and *New York Tyrant*, among others. Recently she completed a crime novel. She teaches at St. Cloud State University.

PHILTRUM

SUDHA BALAGOPAL

After your deployment, after the static-riddled calls, after the thousand-word emails, after you return at Christmas break, after I memorize the indentation above your upper lip, after you say it's called the philtrum—from the Greek for love charm—after the solitude of cold sheets when you leave again, after your helicopter splinters, after your ashes arrive, after he is born, after he's placed in my arms, after I don't want him, after I recognize you in the dip of his upper lip, after I fall in love again, I ask you, why must this beginning come after an ending.

Sudha Balagopal's short fiction is published in *SmokeLong Quarterly*, *Split Lip Magazine* and *Pidgeonholes* among other journals. She is the author of a novel, *A New Dawn*. Her work has been nominated for *The Best Small Fictions*, *Best Microfiction*, the Pushcart Prize and is listed in the *Wigleaf* Top 50.

ETERNAL NIGHT AT THE NATURE MUSEUM, A HALF-HOUR DOWNRIVER FROM THREE MILE ISLAND

TYLER BARTON

On the roof grows a tree Facilities kills every summer. Killed, rather. As the men from Facilities are gone. As everyone—staff, faculty, public—is gone, gone for what Harrisburg still calls temporary. The museum belongs to no one now. Or rather, belongs to that tree, or to the animals and their chewed-through glass, or to the time we lost a snake, every time we lost a snake we couldn't find for days and stayed open for visitors anyway. What I mean is the museum belongs to, I don't know, some kid? The one I sensed hiding in every building I ever closed down for the night. The same kid I imagined stowing away inside the tree trunk, or the shark's mouth, or the trash tote in the mop closet—this milk-mouthed kid with nothing to lose, too spooked to say uncle after having chosen hiding, now living out what was never a Disneyland fantasy but rather the lesser of two let-downs. Life, alone in a building full of owl eggs, appeal letters, revisionist archeology, and arctic wolves who leap like puppies, glass eyes gleaming through their taxidermy. The building belongs to, yes, this starved sapling of a person. And the minute the kid finishes the fish food, cracks two teeth on hematite, retches up the crickets, licks all the pollen from the dead bees' legs—the climbing begins. Up stairs. Up stories. Learning from the lizards who clawed away their cages, this kid will bore with whittled obsidian and patience a hole through the 3rd floor utility door. Behind which lies the ladder, and so, the roof. And so, the tree. And so, the fruit.

Tyler Barton is a literary advocate and cofounder of Fear No Lit. He's the author of a collection of short stories, *Eternal Night at the Nature Museum* (Sarabande Books, 2021) and a chapbook of flash fiction, *The Quiet Part Loud* (Split Lip Press, 2019). Find him @goftyler or tsbarton.com.

THE DINOSAURS THAT DIDN'T DIE

SARAH BATES

I have never left the fields of frozen buffalo. Sometimes a woman is so bound up in the bobbing of
caves, she cannot pull close enough to the water
for sound. I used to cry to the smell of Old Spice
while scrubbing the soap scum off shower heads.
Once in line at a CVS, I picked up the latest issue
of *National Geographic* so I wasn't buying a twelve
pack of condoms alone. Like the first bird, I, too,
have always wanted to gouge the earth, the one
with the plumage on its wings setting off a series of
catastrophic events. I want to get to the part of the
story where the planet is lying down. On page 78,
in the passenger seat of your blue Jeep, I read just
to think of all the ways a person can be kissed. I am
afraid of the places my body will never go. I want
to be jaws bristling, claws out, another solar system
with sharp teeth. I have always felt in my body this
deadliness in being quiet for too long. Sometimes
a woman is afraid of the things that happen that
keep even the oldest birds silent. Picasso was on the
cover and the girl at the cash register laughed and

said something like, "wild night?"

Sarah Bates received an MFA in Creative Writing from Northern Michigan University and currently teaches at Southern Utah University. Her work has appeared or is forthcoming in *Boston Review*, *The Normal School*, and *CutBank*, among others. Her first chapbook, *Tender*, is available from Diagram New Michigan Press.

SHUT YOUR MOUTH AND LISTEN

ROBERTA BEARY

Don't steal my lipstick from my purse and rub it on your lips like a girl, saying lies about chapped lips; *I don't need your stuff now I got my own money, got a phone too*; when you come home from school, put your uniform in the hamper; *the art teacher pays me to pose, Mama, sketches me in charcoal*; put on a clean tee shirt and jeans, don't wear my pink robe ever, my nose can find your sissy smell on my clothes; *teacher calls me his angel, his paradise, calls me Adonis*; when you use the toilet remember do your business quick and don't be lingering, your head in some book of paintings; *teacher says God sent me to him*; when your father visits this weekend, don't let him see you walk like a girl, sit with your back straight; *when I put my clothes back on and I sing, the art teacher says my voice makes the heavens weep*; don't give your father anything to eat or drink, not a crumb, not a sip of water; *Papa says I can visit New York anytime*; you'll grow up like your father, running with strange men; *I'm moving to New York City, soon as I'm 18*; you won't be like him, not as long as I breathe, remember I can see into your soul, no matter what you try and hide; *Papa says you know about me, Mama, he says you've always known.*

Roberta Beary writes to connect with the disenfranchised, to let them know they are not alone. She recently collaborated on The Reluctant Engagement Project, which pairs her writing with artwork by families of people with disabilities. She lives in County Mayo, Ireland with her husband Frank Stella.

PARADE

GARRETT BIGGS

I arrive, I am blindfolded. Wheeled into town. Strapped to the back of a foam dolphin. Everything smells of funnel cake and asphalt. You're promoted, a man says, snapping the blinders off my eyes. His name is Serge. He tells me I came here to celebrate. City of trombones and balloon people and synchronization. Like anyplace else, there's a ladder, a caste system, a mountain or maybe a pecking order. I'm sure there are other metaphors, but you get the picture, he says, flanked by two small children who pull me inside the base of a dog that is not a dog but a balloon we're calling Scooby. The children latch the entrance shut and I row; Scooby lurches forward. You're promoted, Serge shouts from outside. There is some kind of commotion behind the float, a babysitter or a teacher begging someone to stop the procession of brass horns and bodies, but when I open the entrance, the dissent is stifled and Serge is jogging alongside the float. He tosses me a baton and a sequined jumpsuit. They're waiting for me to join the Broadway cast of *Mamma Mia!* A musical that to my knowledge contains no sequined jumpsuits. Have fun with it, he winks, even though people don't wink. But I came here to celebrate. To zip into a sequined jumpsuit. To exhaust myself before the performance is done. And I do exhaust myself before the performance is finished because the performance is never finished. This is a town where Ubers are floats and the floats spell out U.B.E.R. My kneecaps click. My arms throb. You're promoted, Serge says, his fingernails digging into my forearm, filling me with keratin or light or more blood. There is such a thing as promises made, another thing is promises kept, and he promises it's only a matter of time before I'm the Grand Marshal. It's only a few more promotions, he says, before I can finally lead the show.

Garrett Biggs's writing appears in *Black Warrior Review*, *The Rumpus*, *Hayden's Ferry Review*, and *The Offing*, among others. He is managing editor of *The Adroit Journal*, and lives in Denver, Colorado, where he is at work on a novel. Read more at garrettbiggs.net.

FOREST ELEGY

DESPY BOUTRIS

I wasn't the one who started the fire. I was there,
though, in the forest after dark, my unclothed
skin sheened with sweat. It was summer. All of us
smoking, laughing, drunk on our sudden freedom—
no exams, no rules, no one pushing us up against the
wall. Someone rubbed two sticks together, trying to
make sparks. The steady breeze, the chaos of hair.
The arm slung around my waist. A girl and I slunk
deeper into the dark. It was summer. All of us free,
and warm, and full of longing. She touched my face
and I became a burning pine. I touched her thigh
and my hands turned to smoke. I felt a fire spread
through me, and I didn't think about the forest not
about the breeze, the dry heat, the boys playing with
their lighters. I didn't think about the dry grasses,
the pine needles, the gusts of wind threatening to
blow us away. And maybe this is the real risk of
wanting: turning feral, blind to the heat spreading
in the distance, the shouts, the sound of footfall. It
was summer. We were all drunk on freedom. I was
there when the fire spread, running from the flames,
a hand in mine, in our mouths the taste of smoke.

BURIALS

DESPY BOUTRIS

It was the year we buried the rabbit in the backyard.
It was the year of burials, the year of fires and floods
and winds so strong I started walking backwards
and Gas & Electric cut the power to keep telephone
poles from falling and igniting, to keep the whole
town from turning to blaze. I read two books a day
and decided I wanted to break the record for the
world's longest continuous kiss. Or I wanted to turn
scythelike and cut off all that was dead, or to water
this wasteland until it turned green again. My legs
were tree trunks prepared to ignite as smoke spiraled
up toward the sky. That year, I skinny-dipped more
than I care to admit. That year, I dove underwater
unsure if I'd ever come up.

Despy Boutris's work has been published in *Copper Nickel*,
Colorado Review, *American Poetry Review*, *The Gettysburg
Review*, *Prairie Schooner*, and elsewhere. Currently, she teaches
at the University of Houston and serves as Editor-in-Chief of
The West Review.

RAPUNZEL, LET DOWN YOUR

FAYE BRINSMEAD

Hair. Her memories are long green hair. In the morning she winds and binds them. They're heavy, dragging her head down over the desk where she sits, typing words. *I* drifts from sentence to sentence, untethered to her screen-scanning face. *I refer to your email dated. I attach the form for your. I look forward to your early.*

Evenings, alone in her high-rise cubicle, she releases her memories. They ripple down the façade, cover the lower windows with fragrant green silk.

I'll play you something, he says. His fingers tap and fidget, return to her skin. A golden voice spirals the room. Uncoils tiny hairs inside her ears.

What is it? she asks.

Vocalise. Rachmaninov. A song without words. There's only one vowel. Whatever the singer chooses. Which vowel would you choose?

She tries them out.

Ah. Maybe oh.

Pick one, and stick to it, he says. *I'll do it too.*

Oh. Oh. Soft blind sounds, bumping into each other.

One night she comes early, on the off chance. A golden voice sifts through the bricks.

What is it? someone asks.

Vocalise. Rachmaninov. A song without words. There's only one vowel. Whatever the singer chooses. Which vowel would you choose?

Ah. Maybe oh.

Pick one, and stick to it. I'll do it too.

Only the tiny hairs in her ears hear her *oh.*

She keeps its ghost in the green silk. Keeps—that's not quite right. It's never quite the same ghost, quite the same silk.

She rewinds the golden voice, catching different inflections.

Which vowel would you choose?

Ee. Maybe oo.

During the day, she hears the vowels in her long green braid. Trying to reach her *I,* coax it back to life, they call:

Rapunzel, ...

Faye Brinsmead's flash fiction appears in *X-R-A-Y Literary Magazine*, *MoonPark Review*, *New Flash Fiction Review*, and others. She won first prize in *Reflex Fiction*'s Spring 2020 flash fiction competition and has been nominated for the Pushcart Prize. She lives in Australia and tweets @ContesdeFaye.

I'VE SEEN BIGGER

LORI SAMBOL BRODY

I'm still angry, but I agree to hunt scorpions with my husband. He thinks it'll be fun to use the blacklight I got him for his birthday. Maybe he'll apologize. Our yard borders onto the state park, the light of the full moon silhouetting jagged branches of oaks and bleaching the dry grass clogging the seasonal creek. The beam of his blacklight shines a purple circle on fallen oak galls and brightens the white pet headstones. We walk in silence; soon he'll say, *I didn't mean it*, at least that's what I imagine. *Here's one*, he whispers. On the oak duff, a small scorpion shines an aggressive blue-green. The front pinchers, the segmented body like beads. *I've seen bigger*, I say. It's scorpion season: one fell on me yesterday from the bedroom ceiling. *We need to go deeper*, he says. Between our property and the state park, he'd built a wood fence with a gate when the twins were just toddlers. Beyond the gate, a copse of coast live oak and a vast meadow slope uphill. *Don't go past the gate*, I always told the twins. When I look back at our house, two shadows, mirroring the other's movements, move across a brightly-lit window in the twin's room: they must be recording TikTok dance videos. My husband opens the creaking gate and I follow him through the oaks. Tree roots protrude like arthritic fingers. His blacklight snares another scorpion, mouse-sized. It freezes then burrows into the duff. We continue into the meadow, through reeds swaying without wind. He says, *We need to go deeper.* I can't see our house anymore. The meadow spreads on forever, my husband's blacklight arcing the ground before us. I've been following him for so long and he still has not apologized. He points out more scorpions, each larger than the last, as big as a rat, a house cat, a skunk. *Are they supposed to be that big*, I say, and he says, *Scorpions are of various sizes.* We now walk under trees, not any native species I recognize, the trunks growing so close that dark latticed branches become the sky. My anger hangs between us. He sweeps the blacklight again and I see a scorpion glowing. The size of a coyote. Tail curled, stinger dripping with venom. The whites of my husband's eyes gleam and he says, *We need to go deeper.*

Lori Sambol Brody is a Scorpio and has gone scorpion hunting with her husband, but never while angry. Her short fiction has appeared in *The Rumpus*, *SmokeLong Quarterly*, *Wigleaf*, *CRAFT*, *The Best Small Fictions* 2018 and 2019 anthologies, and elsewhere.

IT'S 5 AM-ISH, AND MY FATHER TELLS ME A STORY FROM HIS TIME IN SINGAPORE

EXODUS OKTAVIA BROWNLOW

I am riding along with my father in a too-dirty pickup truck, in a pair of grey sweatpants, in a bleach-stained Bruno Mars T-shirt, and there's a bonnet on my head that keeps the hair-rollers underneath in place, still.

He says, "When I was in the Navy, over there in Singapore, there was only two things the people ever asked you—"

It is 5 am-ish in the morning, and the sky is just beginning to become.

I note how not-sleepy I am, how if I really wanted to get up at 5 am, every day, to achieve some semblance of the success that folks who wake up at this hour have, I probably could.

"They ask," and he assumes an accent. One that I should reprimand him for, but I tell myself that I'll get to it later. I forget to get to it later. *Have you ever been to California? Do you know Michael Jackson?*"

27

He has been telling me these Navy stories since I was a kid.

- His first time getting seriously drunk in Japan from something called Red Monkey.

- His religious transition from Christianity to Islam, and how when he'd wanted to study the Quran, it always had to be done in a locked room, away from the rest of the texts deemed safe enough for free, public domain.

- His relief in being a young black Mississippi man, and finding similar souls on the ship who too were young, black, male and hailed from states like Alabama, Georgia, and The Carolinas. *Y'all*, being the common pronoun.

As an almost 28-year-old, this story is very new.

"And I told them, *Yeah, I been to California. Yeah, I know Michael Jackson ... know him personally!*"

I don't ask him why he lied about the Michael Jackson thing, mainly because I am in love with the why that I've created.

It's nice to be nice, and it's very nice to feel like you know someone who's been to all the places, who's shaken hands with the world's most influential people.

It's nice to preserve some small inkling of the child

that lives inside of us all, where believing in the impossibility of every story is safe, and wonderful.

It is 6 am-ish, and the sky has become.

The cantaloupe cream orange pours into the angel-whipped white.

The iced-baby-blues, the blackened-seal-teals, serves as their bowl.

Exodus Oktavia Brownlow is a Blackhawk, MS native. She has been published with *Electric Literature*, *Hobart*, *Booth*, *Fractured Lit*, *Jellyfish Review*, and more. She is currently working on her novel. Exodus loves the color green.

ON HESITATION

TAYLOR BYAS

I wished I'd let you drive as the sky closed the lid
on things. The headlights on the other side of the
highway blurred to orbs as fuzzy as dandelions, my
sight failing in the dark. But I was in a groove, wasn't
ready to stop again before we crossed the next state
line. So when you spotted a barn—a black stamp
licked and pressed against the midnight blue—I
stopped you before you even began. *We don't have
time for adventures.* But this pattern continued, you
straightening at each sighting of wood-rot, at every
front barn door cracked open like a knife wound.
Soon, I tired of the cornfields. Their sameness, the
vanity with which they continued to spawn the self.
So I indulged you, abandoned the highway's smooth
to spit gravel in the wake of your Jeep. When we
pulled up to this barn, you dated its abandonment.
At least 10, 15 years, because of the smile of the
roof. The wind breezing through the barn's gut, its
cat-call whistle, and both sets of doors blown open.
Your pulse two-stepped during our silent watching
and I thought you were turned on by this somehow.
And my God, you were. *Let's go in. Find some hay,*

like in the movies. And what of the pessimist in me?
Betting on the rustic charm of disarray as a trap,
some chainsaw-wielding killer eyeing us from the
cyclops window. Even you could go rogue, one bite of
me giving way to another, then another. But you've
gotten out of the car now, come around and opened
my door. *We'll laugh about this years from now.* Your
hand in the dark not how I've always remembered it.

Taylor Byas is a Black Chicago native living in Cincinnati, Ohio.
She is a second year PhD student at the University of Cincinnati.
She was the 1st place winner of the Poetry Super Highway
and the Frontier Poetry Award for New Poets Contests. Her
chapbook, *Bloodwarm*, is forthcoming in 2021.

A WORLD BEYOND CARDBOARD

JONATHAN CARDEW

Mum died, so Dad took us on a holiday to France. Brittany, to be specific. The Côtes-d'Armor. A nothing town called Lancieux, nestled into a crumbling cliff.

Pretty for about five minutes.

Jess and I played: *Stick our noses in our phones for as long as we can.*

Dad played: *Binge-listen to Seventies songs on my old-ass iPod.*

Inspiration struck.

"Let's walk the walls. We're gonna walk the walls," Dad said, pulling out his earphones.

Dad marched out in front, keen to catch every angle. He touched the walls, breathed in the salt air.

The walls rose out of the water. Big, thick ones. Meant to repel invaders—not doing a very good job then.

Generally, Dad tried too hard.

In a café on a slanted street, we drank coffee and

watched street performers.

Dad slowed down.

Each of his sips was a journey.

We hung off each one, hoping he would say something of substance.

Just say some thing.

In front of us, a puppeteer dropped his puppets into a cardboard theatre, and the growing crowd laughed as the miniature people acted out an ordinary family scene: the father, with his diminutive briefcase, arriving home from the office; the mother, preparing a meal at a tiny stove; the daughters, playing with their own very small puppets, oblivious to the crowd around them, to a world beyond cardboard.

The mother puppet paused, threw down a dish rag the size of a coin.

We watched her, hardly breathing.

Originally from the UK, Jonathan Cardew now calls the Midwest his home. His stories appear in *Cream City Review*, *Passages North*, *Wigleaf*, *SmokeLong Quarterly*, and others. He tweets @cardewjcardew.

HALF MOON BAY

K-MING CHANG

When Yeye died, I drove with my wife to see the bay at low-tide, the sea baring its black teeth. Once, Yeye said the moon was born in two. Light lives to seek its mortal half, flipping our faces like coins to find the one it completes. When they called to tell me, my sisters were sharing a phone, speaking the word so slow it was two, *de* & *ad*, their teeth grinding into salt. He said once: the moon is a man who will marry you someday. At the bay, my wife calls to me in a language he never knew. Her mouth around my name: the moon.

ASYMMETRY

K-MING CHANG

I cut my mother's hair every month since her hands went wild. They're rabid, boomeranging around the room, returning every touch twice as hard, slapping her face when she's asleep, ambushing mosquitoes, crawling under the sofa like rodents. I cut her hair shorter in the front than in the back. She likes asymmetry, the unevenness of things. She claims that's why she fell in love with my father. He had one eye that was double-lidded and one that was single-lidded, one smaller than the other, which my mother called long-feng yan. Dragon-phoenix eyes. A sign of good luck. Eyes like coins, like currency, spending themselves empty. Every month, I spray my mother's hair from the roots to the tips, trace the cowlick on her scalp, trim away the bleached-brittle ends. Unlike her, I prefer symmetry. I cut my own hair in a bob so abrupt that my friends call me a cartoon character. I like straight lines, pleats, windows that are perfectly square, cornered light. I don't like things that hinge or open by themselves, like doors or mouths or pasts. The woman who taught me at cosmetology school had a haircut like my mother's: asymmetrical, red highlights, bangs dangling over one eye. One day in class, she volunteered to be my practice-customer. I kept looking at her face in the mirror instead of at her hair, at my own hands, and so I nicked her by accident. The left ear-tip. I touched my tongue to her ear, sucked away the blood. It was instinct, I told her later, but she still expelled me. Said I needed to learn limits. How could I explain that whenever I saw blood, I could only imagine it inside my own mouth. That once, days after I spoke back to my father and he slapped me, one of my eyes was swollen shut and the other remained open, how I couldn't bear to look at the asymmetry of my eyes in the mirror, one dragon, one phoenix, wondering what woman could fall in love with looking this way.

K-Ming Chang / 張欣明 is a Kundiman fellow, a Lambda Literary Award finalist, and a National Book Foundation 5 Under 35 honoree. She is the author of the debut novel *Bestiary* (One World). Her short story collection, *Resident Aliens*, is forthcoming. More of her writing is at kmingchang.com.

WINDOWS

RANJABALI CHAUDHURI

I love shop windows. Their colours, jewels, and mannequins sing the dulcet promise of possibility. They let me be anyone. Superimposed upon the clothes on display, my reflection can be a soldier in a red and gold jacket, a doctor in a white coat with deep pockets or even a gentleman in a gray suit, a red silk scarf and a cream hat. They take my imagination to places I am not allowed to enter. I wish they were the only windows I had to clean.

The pastries look delicious, but I cannot linger. The bungalow has ten windows, framed in painted glass. The *sahibs* and *memsahibs* inside do not like to keep them open for long. A servant follows me to keep my hands from straying inside. Everything native is banned within these four walls—the heat, the dust, the words, the people. I steal quick glances of this life made of pastries, pianos, and porcelain. These windows scream at me to work faster, to collect my wages and disappear. Wasps buzz over the white roses that grow on their sills.

It is dark when I reach the club. A man browner than me, wearing the club's black uniform, points me to the only place where a brown boy with a bucket is allowed. I smile and run. I have been waiting for these windows all day long. Music from inside floats in the air. The *sahibs* have parked their cars in three neat rows. I use the cloth that hides the contents of my bucket to cover my shirt. Paint spills from a tin I open. I pick a brush and look at the English words our leader has written down for me, at the bottom of my bucket. One word for each window.

Quit India

Jai Hind

Ranjabali Chaudhuri's (she / her) work has appeared in *FlashBack Fiction*, *The Timeworn Literary Journal*, and *The Horla Magazine* among others. She lives in London and is working on her first novel.

FLOATERS

ANNE COOPERSTONE

"So my dad is rich," Walt said. "So what? I still think we should eat them."

"What? Eat what?" Polly said.

She tried to get a good look at him, but the sun made her squint. They were in a two-person raft, floating down the Boise River in late July.

"Eat the rich," Walt said. He took a swig of his Apple Orchard. He'd put zinc on his nose and the rim of the cider bottle was stained white. After a moment of silence, Walt said, "What, you've never heard of that?"

"No, I have," Polly said, lying back onto the raft, watching her hip bones jut out in that way she'd always liked.

Other rafts floated by. One carried a family with screeching kids and ziplock baggies of sandwiches, another a solo rafter with a scuba mask and a farmer's tan.

Polly should have lost Walt's number after their first date. It'd been a total bust. They'd gone for dumplings at a roof top restaurant, but they left before the cart came around; swarms of flies were hovering at eye level, swelling around the hot string lights that lined the patio, landing on their cheeks and tongues until their appetites were gone. There was a version of the night that could have been romantic. Last minute tickets to the drive-in, or scoops from the Ben and Jerry's by the mall. Instead, they'd just gone home.

Their raft bumped up against a rock and they jostled hard. Polly heard Walt's bottle crack against his teeth.

"Ow." He bared his teeth at Polly. His front right tooth was missing a tiny corner. "Is it bleeding?"

"I don't think so."

"That really hurt," he said, touching his lip gingerly. "Anyway. What was I saying?"

"Your dad," Polly said.

Maybe she'd call that guy tonight, she thought, the one who'd let her ride his motorcycle without a helmet. The wind had made her chest feel full. As Walt chattered on, she let her fingers drift against the babbling rapids, some big, some small.

Anne Cooperstone is a current MFA candidate in creative writing at Stony Brook Southampton and a recipient of the Graduate Council Fellowship. She is based in New York City.

GHOUL

NOA COVO

We feed the ghoul behind the elementary school crumbs of bread and throw sticks at it to make it dance. We watch its grotesque movements, our heads ducked down, squinting in fear, until our mothers call us for dinner, garbled words painting a language that skips down the street and rings in our ears. We cringe as foreign words sneak in, marring the pictures we have painted for ourselves on the walls of the elementary school, our language in big block letters, our parents' language woven in the cracks of the pavement. Our mothers tell us to eat until there is nothing on our plates and we sneak what's left into our pockets.

Our mothers ask us where we've been over dinner and we mumble names, our mothers shake their heads and tell us, don't spend time with them. We know the rest of us are being told this as well. We know each of our mothers think all of the other mothers are crazy and we know that our mothers know we have discovered the ghoul and we gather crumbs of bread, of shaking hands, of voices whispered in the night, of letters that roll wrong on our parents'

41

tongues and we slip all of it into our pockets. We feed the ghoul and we eat what is left so that one day we will be big enough and strong enough to watch it dance without turning away.

Noa Covo's work has been published in or is forthcoming from *Jellyfish Review*, *Waxwing* and *Passages North*. Her micro-chapbook, *Bouquet of Fears*, was published by Nightingale and Sparrow Press. She can be found on Twitter @covo_noa.

THERE ARE FRIJOLES PINTOS LOST INSIDE THE SOFA

MOISÉS R. DELGADO

Frijoles lost in the brown carpet. Frijoles blending into our brown palms. The frijol with the snake-like pattern. Our preferred frijol. Frijoles I eat on white bread for breakfast, dinner, and sometimes as a night snack because I am a picky eater, but frijoles always sit well on my tongue. Frijoles we use to play lotería on Saturday nights. We scatter them on our playing boards and the frijoles look like frijol-shaped stars, their shells reflecting light into our frijol-brown eyes. There is no frijol card to be called, but there is La Luna. And what's a crescent moon but a frijol reflecting the sun's light down into our frijol-hungry eyes? Dad holds his sixteen frijoles in the hand not raising the beer to his lips. And Mom holds one at a time, kneads the frijol with freshly manicured fingers. *¿Must you keep drinking?* she says and pinches the frijol like it's a rosary she is tired of praying with. Dad rattles the frijoles in his fist and says it's all for fun—*Let me have fun, ¿won't you?* The curtains are open, so across the

43

street, and beneath the star-shaped frijoles in the blue cooking pot of a sky, we can see the neighbors have also gathered in their living room. And they can see us: figures kneeling over lotería boards and frijoles. Mom reaches for Dad's fourth beer and he spills his frijoles to try and save it, but his spirits fall and are soaked up by his lotería board. The frijoles only float in the alcohol for a second before they sink and are lost in the carpet. Inside that second, frijoles mid-float and frijoles mid-sink, Mom starts crying. In that second, a frijol of sweat beads on Dad's Cupid bow and he drowns it with a swig of a fifth Bud Light. Somewhere within the one second, a frijol-shaped something is lost and lodged in my head, only to be found, like with all lost things, when something else is lost.

Moisés R. Delgado is a Latinx writer from the Midwest. He is an MFA candidate at the University of Arizona. His prose appears in *The Pinch*, *Puerto del Sol*, *Passages North*, *Pidgeon-holes*, *Homology Lit*, *X-R-A-Y Literary Magazine*, and elsewhere. When not writing, Moisés can be found dancing on the moon.

MATT'S BASEMENT

LEONORA DESAR

I ask Matt if we can move into his basement. Technically, it's his father's basement. Technically, Matt still lives in it. Technically, Matt is 32 years old. But what is technicality? I present the following cost-benefit analysis.

Costs: Nothing!

We're living in his father's basement.

Benefits:

- Free food
- Free pizza
- Free donuts
- Free sex (that would be from each other)

The feeling of utter privacy / cloisterization coupled with parental care. Whenever we are not getting enough love (from each other) we retreat to the Kingdom of Upstairs, where we can watch football with Matt's dad. Problem of emptiness and unsupervision solved! What do you think?

Matt tells me he'll have to think about it. In the meantime can we hang out?

Where?

In the basement.

We hang out. He smells like pineapple. This was a smell that he was born with, I'm convinced of this. For the rest of his life he's been in serious denial. No, I do not smell like pineapple. I smell like used condoms and sex on the beach and Marlboro cigarettes, and sometimes a wistful sadness, a melancholy, like James Dean from the grave. It's why the basement smells. Not like James Dean though, Fruit Roll-Ups. Also our disintegration—

He lies with his arms around me. They seem to say, we can stay like this forever. We do not have to be Old. We do not have to get jobs that we'll then be fired from and go Upstairs (where Matt's dad will ask us when we're getting new ones)—

We can stay like this. We can even have Children. They will have skipped the Basement Gene. We'll raise them here, and when they're ready we'll tell them about the bad place—Outside. They will be responsible citizens and get jobs and provide for their ailing parents. They'll go Upstairs and then to the Upstairs Beyond, otherwise known as The Office. They will Succeed. We will read about them in the papers, which Matt's dad will deliver, very old now and very feeble. They will bring Grandchildren. We will dote on them, and remark how they smell like pineapple. How they do nothing to get in its way.

SOME MEANING—

LEONORA DESAR

Every day the alarm would go off and every day I'd wait to feel some Meaning. Maybe today, I'd say. Maybe today is finally the day.

I'd go to work and still not find it. Then my boss would say, Here you go. Some Meaning. I'd reach out and take it, but it was only coffee. Or tea. Or sometimes a bad donut / pencil. So I'd bend over and show him my lace underwear. He liked it—

He'd bend me over the desk and look for Meaning. He'd say, There is something in your thighs or in that freckle there, but when he inspected closer, he couldn't find it, and then we'd go to Burger Heaven and have some lunch—

He had a wife. Two kids. He was still waiting for Meaning. Then he told me the truth—that it was never going to happen. His only chance was getting to the Top. He'd spend the entire day climbing, when he wasn't at Burger Heaven or checking out my underwear.

He said that I should focus too. He handed me the Corporate Ladder. It was brown and ropey; he told me that it stretched. That I should climb. One foot then the other. I could even do it in place. Or during lunch. Or even while showing him my underwear. Or even while asleep—

And I spent hours too—

Searching in his ear, or in his cheekbone. In the long curve of his cock. I'd whisper to it, Are you Meaningful, and it said, Yes. *Yes*. I looked for it in his smell, dandelions mixed with orchids that he borrowed from his wife. Maybe *she* was the Meaningful one. I called her up and asked, Maybe you can give me Meaning? Sorry, she said, I cannot, and can you stop fucking my husband?

But I could not. We spent hours at the Burger Heaven. We ordered french fries. Hamburgers. Coleslaw. We looked for meaning in sour dill pickles and in the raw pink bellies of fried pork. In the waitress's green slanted eyes, in the way that she tenderly took our food orders. In the way her breath rose, like she had just finished a race.

Leonora Desar's writing has appeared in *The Cincinnati Review*, *No Contact*, *River Styx*, and *Columbia Journal*, where she was chosen as a finalist by Ottessa Moshfegh. Her work was selected for *The Best Small Fictions* 2019, the *Wigleaf* Top 50 (2019 and 2020), and *Best Microfiction* 2019 and 2020.

SOMETHING LIKE HAPPY

EMILY DEVANE

I came here with a body full of poison and hair loose in its sockets. The thrill of standing by the harbour is something else. *Better than Disneyland*, you say. *Of course*, I reply, *of course*.

Gulls screech like newborn babes and the air has a taste to it like sweat, like tears, like life at its gritty best. And we say yes: to ice cream with sprinkles and sky-blue candyfloss; to hours of digging holes in the sand and skipping over the waves, our skin staying just the right side of pink, our lungs stinging, singing with the salt; to crabbing beside the harbour wall; to feeding our twopenny pieces into the metal-guzzling machines at the arcade, watching the forwards and backwards until they're all gone.

By the caravan with the genuine Romany inside, I wonder if, with one look, she'll avert her eyes, knowing my fate.

We climb the steps and I'm breathless but I don't make a fuss because today is an illusion and it matters, more than anything, to be normal.

A stranger takes a photograph of us in the picture-postcard cemetery, its tombstones rakish as ageing teeth. Our faces beam with the relief of the fearful. For now, we are saying, this is okay, this can be done. And though the wind whips my hair into tangled knots and my scalp tingles with the losses to come and my life is too short to count, we are something like happy, and that is enough.

Emily Devane is a writer, teacher and editor from Ilkley, West Yorkshire. Her work is widely published and has won prizes, including the Bath Flash Fiction Award, a Northern Writers' Award and a Word Factory Apprenticeship. Emily is an editor at *FlashBack Fiction*. She teaches at Moor Words (@WordsMoor).

WHEN WE WERE YOUNG

CHRISTOPHER M. DREW

we'd cut school and crowd the narrow bridge over the railroad, all of us together, while behind us the signalman would open the small window of his hut and bellow, *Careful there, lads, step back now*, but we'd laugh and on tiptoe lean over the iron railings, our loose shirttails folding up in the breeze and flakes of rust-green paint crumbling between our fingers, and soon our bones would tremble with a sound like deep thunder and our hearts would merge with the sure beat of the wheels hammering forward and in a blink it would be upon us, screaming like the death rattle of a blazing phoenix, sweeping inches beneath our feet, and in that moment we'd raise our arms as though we were soaring through a towering storm cloud, thrown about by a fierce wind, spiraling out of control, and we'd blink the soot from our eyes, black tears streaming down our dazed faces, and disappear into the whorl of thick smoke billowing around us, and when the smoke cleared we'd stand there, breathless, the taste of sulphur sharp and gritty in our mouths, until the last fragile wisps had dissolved into the clean golden light breaking through the stirred trees, then the signalman would shout, *Move along now, lads, move along*, and we'd shoulder our bags and in silence cross the bridge, each of us heading our separate ways home.

Christopher M. Drew is a writer from Sheffield, UK. His flash fiction has appeared in places such as *The Forge Literary Magazine*, *Splonk*, *Lunate Fiction*, *trampset*, and *SmokeLong Quarterly*. You can connect with Chris on Twitter @cmdrew81, or through his website https://chrisdrew81.wixsite.com/cmdrew81.

PLACES I HAVE PEED

EPIPHANY FERRELL

1. The Grand Canyon, hiding behind a mule, during a break on the overnight trip to the Phantom Ranch. I was 16 and mortified.

2. Hoover Dam, the restroom on top of the dam with an intriguing Deco design on the floor. I was 22 and high as a kite.

3. At Tony's, where Jordan asked me to marry him. Try the tenderloin with *foie gras*. It is to die for, I swear.

4. The Larimore, with my bridesmaids, two of them, holding my tulle and satin and lace moments before I was to make my grand entrance.

5. My in-laws' timeshare in Naples, Florida, where the bathroom was decorated with mermaid tiles and a claw-foot bathtub painted pearly aquamarine.

6. The Gulf of Mexico, several times, on our honeymoon.

7. My in-laws' house in the country, the bathroom at the back of the house where I borrowed without asking a Zoloft from the array of neatly arranged choices.

8. Same place, on a magic stick that showed a plus sign.

9. The Chicago penthouse where I hid in the Jacuzzi tub (empty) until Jordan and a brunette I vaguely remembered from our wedding went onto the balcony and I crept away with a pair of red panties found on the floor.

Epiphany Ferrell lives perilously close to the Shawnee Hills Wine Trail in Southern Illinois. Her stories appear in *Ghost Parachute*, *New Flash Fiction Review*, *Dead Mule School of Southern Literature*, *Miracle Monacle* and other places. She is a two-time Pushcart nominee.

WHAT THE DREAMING TOWN SAYS TO YOU, YOU IN THIS *ONLY* LOVE

PAT FORAN

When the town feels like talking, it talks about the darkness— "it's there and it's there, and there, and there," the town says. It talks about the cold in cursive, in a spacesuit, under a day-for-night moon.

You and I are talking, too. We're talking together, we're sleeping together, we're talking without sleeping. Talking without telling, talking without telling anyone anything. Not about the masquerading moon, not about this spacesuited town. Not about us, this *only* us. Not here, in the dark, in this cold, on this night.

"Something there is about this darkness," we say to each other. It's the kind of darkness that flies a kite without a key tied to its tail. The kind that surprises you with cattails and bulrushes on your birthday. The kind you write song lyrics about on the inside of her left arm, along the vein lines, in a time signature only she can feel.

This cold. Its color. How it doesn't run, *won't* run. The *shush* of it. The *us* in it. How we miss it, how we miss us, this *only* us, when it starts to get warm.

This night. How it scales Mount Perception when possibility nestles in the night's cliffs like an isotope that's half in love. How sure it is, this possibility. Cocksure. How sure *we* are. Sure as we're sitting (and not sleeping) here.

This *closeness*. Closer than colorfast, faster than falling in Twitter love. How awkward it would be, this colorfasting, this falling, if it weren't so freakin' dark. If we weren't so geeked-out giddy because we're able to talk this way, together, in this *only* love.

This town—it's sheepish, with certainty in its step, and blood in its bootstraps. A town without power chords, a town without pity. A town *without*. A town, in a spacesuit, that talks about springtime, sings about summer, and dreams about the only people not sleeping. The only ones not shivering. Especially when the not sleeping ones say, to each other, in the dark, in this cold, on this night: *As if* and *If only*.

"Welcome to our town," the dreaming town says to us, only. "Aren't we beautiful when we shiver? Aren't we beautiful when we sleep? Aren't we beautiful?"

Pat Foran is a writer in Milwaukee, Wisconsin. His work has appeared in various journals, including *Tahoma Literary Review*, *Milk Candy Review*, *Wigleaf*, *WhiskeyPaper* and elsewhere.

INSTRUCTIONS FOR CLEANING A MIRROR

SARAH FRELIGH

I have my secrets. I take my time, stare at my face until I'm a stranger, a she who is not me. A she who helps herself to whatever will buff the sharp edges of the world. Yesterday a yellow pill pinned the sun to the center of the sky where it remained unstained by clouds. Waiting for the bus, she danced to the thunder of drums from a car idling at a red light. A glass door gave her back herself, a whirling dervish in sneakers. If you drove by just then you'd think, *now there's a happy gal.*

Sarah Freligh is the author of *We* and *Sad Math*, winner of the 2014 Moon City Press Poetry Prize and the 2015 Whirling Prize from the University of Indianapolis. She is the recipient of a poetry fellowship from the National Endowment for the Arts.

ALICE IN VORELAND

LAUREN FRIEDLANDER

To eat my love the way she always dreamt, either she had to get smaller or I bigger. Porn she liked was big broads, fifty-footers sort of big, queen kongs, skyscraper-legged and black-hole-mouthed to hoover up lovers the size of mites. Porn I liked was—no matter.

Decided was we drew straws. The straw decided: I, Alice, Bigger.

I could not dwell. I swallowed quickly pride, and pills, overnighted from a site (Amazons) that specialized in such sexual bents.

My love said Trust me. What choice had I?

These strange effects took no sweet time. I bigged all right, hundredfold. Broke the house on through! Right arm filled the master bath, left leg wrecked the drive. Skull met with reclaimed beams where the sun beat in, plaster like confetti down my hair the mile long. I stood, and thus standing, darkened the town.

At spurt's end—was it end? Would it ever be?— my love marveled me up and down and fairly. I was a thing to marvel. Straddling my pinky nail, her chirp demanded from a great distance: GO! and IN!

I swallowed her, most specialest pill, as she begged of me in dreams. Her final act: the happy shriek of eatenness, the last of her. She tasted of, well, nothing. Not teatree shampoo, not chicken. Within the day I'd passed her. She exited the other side in a cocoon of waste, dead of course but smiles all over, as ever, ever on this rictus in the muck. Her fantasy so quickly wrung, most happiest death. Wasn't it? What she asked of me? Didn't I?

I remain. Here. My days of largesse pass like velvet curtains ever-parting from a play without end, and I unaudienced. And there she, joy voided in the earth's commode—happy? Oh, dear, what choice had I. With bloated fingers thick as blimps I mark her little spot to ward off urinating dogs and reckless kids, though already all steer clear of the lone giantess of the plains. Clumsily—but hopefully!—as I now maneuver all my days—I plant this pack of seeds. I water, tend, and hope; so as not to galumph, defile, or barge. Come spring, with any luck at all, my hyacinth girl.

Lauren Friedlander is a writer from Kansas living in Brooklyn. She was a recipient of the 2018 PEN / Robert J. Dau Short Story

Prize for Emerging Writers and has fiction published or forth-coming in *Catapult*, *Washington Square Review*, *The Rumpus*, and elsewhere. She is currently at work on a novel. www.laurenfriedlander.net.

LOST MEMORY

JEFF FRIEDMAN

My sister stole a memory of mine from my house and took it home, hidden in her coat. I couldn't remember the memory, but there was an empty space on the sideboard under the window. "Give me back the memory," I said, standing outside her door. "And I won't report you to the authorities." She let me in. "Don't be ridiculous," she said. "Why would I steal a memory of yours?" It didn't take me long to find the memory, a blue jar sitting on the glass stand between two chairs. When I picked it up, she looked puzzled. "This is my place," she said. "These are my things." "Not true," I replied and unscrewed the lid. Emptiness wafted out with its stinging scent. Now I remembered something I had wanted to forget. I screwed the lid back on quickly and set it down. "That's my memory," she said. "You shouldn't have opened it." "Then what do you remember?" I asked. "Nothing—it's gone because you let it out." And as I stood there, angry at my sister, the scent of the memory evaporated, and all I could remember was the jar, and now that belonged to her.

NOT EVERYTHING WAS IN MY FATHER'S WILL

JEFF FRIEDMAN

My father left me a CD with nothing in it and
a record of all his closed accounts. He left me a hole
in which to deposit old birds, the bust of the uncle
he hated, old newspaper clippings of ads for clothing
lines he was selling, the transistor radio he pressed
to his ear to hear the ballgames, tales of his early
days tossing feed to the chickens and chasing after
the cow that wandered off into the field, the words
to songs he no longer remembered, but still tried
to sing. He left me a bridge to Paris the size of
a chipmunk and a deed to a parcel of land on Mars.
He left me the lingering scent of the Wildroot Hair
Oil he combed through his thin wavy hair every
morning. He left me the shadows inside his closet,
waiting for the venetian blinds to be opened at dawn.
He left me three pairs of glossy black wingtips and
the sound of their shuffling over the sidewalks. He
left me a leather jacket that held the shape of his
round belly pressed against its buttons. He left me
an envelope of Kennedy half dollars, each a talisman
against curses and bad luck. He left me the country

of hope floating in his brown eyes, the broken tree of his Hungarian ancestors, his favorite cliché about the past, "That's ancient history"—and his hunger for heavy stews.

Jeff Friedman's eighth book, *The Marksman*, was published in November 2020 by Carnegie Mellon University Press. He has received numerous awards and prizes for his poetry, mini tales, and translations, including a National Endowment Literature Translation Fellowship in 2016 and two individual Artist Grants from New Hampshire Arts Council.

SHE'S GONE

FRANCES GAPPER

Together my wife Mary and I built a snowman. We gave it eyes and a mouth of stone, a carrot stub of a nose.

Mary asked me to take a snap. She posed with her chin on the snowman's head, her hand on its breast. The snowman looked a bit embarrassed. It leaned away from her.

I said it's nice to see you looking happy and rosy cheeked. Added I love you. But she only stared at me with her pebble-grey eyes.

Next morning, thaw. Oh, Mary said, she's gone.

Was it a she then, I asked.

Frances Gapper currently lives in the UK's Black Country region. Her flashes and micros can be seen in e.g. *Under the Radar*, *Meniscus*, *The Cafe Irreal*, *Wigleaf*, *The Ilanot Review*, *The Citron Review*, *New Flash Fiction Review*, *The Phare*, *Splonk* and *Spelk*.

THE CORRECT HANGING OF GAME BIRDS

ROSIE GARLAND

Rostrum

Select old, wild birds. Beware harsh beaks, horned spurs, claws toughened by years of defiance. Pierce the beak. Hang by the neck, the feet. Each man has his taste. Hook and hang them long enough to conquer disobedience.

Pectoral girdle

Keep them in the dark. Convert the cellar into a hanging room: a stamped dirt floor to absorb the moisture they shrug off, dense walls to absorb sound. Keep your birds separate. Even when dead, their warmth communicates from breast to breast, stirring discord.

Syrinx

Permit yourself the luxury of appreciation. This bird is yours, now. Dawdle on the ruffled collar, handsome as a rope of pearls around the throat; eye ringed with the purple-blue of bruising; jewel plumage so thick it weighs down the wings. You can't imagine how she flapped or flew.

Breast

Pluck right away and you experience the thrill of naked flesh, but the body will dry out. Your bird is ruined. Wait three days, maybe seven. Then and only then, strip off the feathers. Patience. Flesh and innards need time to ripen. Sublime flavour is attained when skin loosens its grasp on muscle. She oozes oil and perfume.

Rump

A gentle incision. Slice skin, not meat. Slide in up to the wrist and spread your fingers. Unpeel her body like wet fruit. Relish satin texture, the greenish shimmer of perfect ripeness. Keep going. Fillet scraps from bone, a job less bloody than you expect. Persistence rewarded with flesh that yields to your authority.

Lesser coverts

Lock the dog in the yard, to stop it lapping up the puddles that collect under the carcasses. Ignore the neighbours complaining they can't sleep. The smile that shuts them up faster than any bellowed argument. The way they shrink away.

Cloaca

Time passes without needing to pay it much

attention. Nights in the cellar, waiting for your birds. Their toes dripping, their eyes glazed. All resistance drained from them. The silence is balm, the scent delectable and rare. If only the dog would stop barking.

Writer and singer with post-punk band The March Violets, Rosie Garland's award-winning work has been published internationally. Her new poetry collection *What Girls Do in the Dark* (Nine Arches Press) is out now. In 2019, Val McDermid named her one of the UK's most compelling LGBT+ writers.

JUNK

SCOTT GARSON

I'd like to think my father feels the weakness of the line he gives about why he's set aside a stack of junk mail addressed to my dead name. You might need it, he says. I don't know what's in there. I might need a father also, I don't say. Because pointlessness. In truth, the father in him has been pledged to a social security number, to an idea of a person whose interests would seem to include flooring and discount garden supplies. Competitive cable providers. I neaten the stack. I can feel its loose edge in my palm. *Congratulations!* one envelope says.

Scott Garson is the author of *Is That You, John Wayne?*—a collection of stories. He lives in central Missouri.

BEATING THE HERRING

MARIE GETHINS

Cross to shoulder, you bear the burden, sleeves covered in white fragments. A single herring remains. It trembles, glinting silver, then gold in the Easter Morning light. The river beckons.

Earlier, a row of penitent fish hung on the cross above your head. Eyes to heaven, their forked tails rigid in death. The crowd shouted and swung sticks: knocking scales, flesh from bone. A swirling dance to the fiddler's lurid tune. Herring splinters rained down onto your black tricorne. I kept your indigo coat in sight, while floating through drunks and laughing matrons. Jostled, but never faltering in your wake, my new bonnet muffled the din.

You are my Lamb. You take away...

At Cork's North Gate, you brush flakes of white and bits of metallic skin off your shoulders into the swift Lee flow. A single fish soul left intact. You search through heads and hats to catch my gaze. We exchange smiles.

The lamb quarter arrives on a butcher's back. You tie it beneath the fish, onto the lath, crown it with my ribbons. Cheers erupt as it is hoisted high. Red and blue banners flutter on the breeze and the fiddler saws a new refrain.

Da pushes his way out of the eddying mob, a thick rod raised. The old pounding fills my ears, its rhythmic beat drowns out the crowd. You seek my eyes again and give a gentle nod. "Stay, my love."

You are my Lamb. You take away...

With whiskey and sweat, Da used to come in darkness, leaving me with another smell. Now you face him, lift the cross again to lead the crowd along Bachelors Quay into the City. Above a sea of heads, the tiny herring quivers in the sun. Da strikes at it, but hits the meat that hangs below. The lamb remains solid, does not yield. Untouched, the fish sways, a jewel in the spring glow. The crowd laughs around us, taunts him. He is nothing. I push past his red face to walk beside you and my heart swims free.

Marie Gethins' flash appeared in *Banshee*, *NFFD* anthologies, *Flash*, *Jellyfish Review*, *Litro*, *FlashBack Fiction*, *NANO*, *Fictive Dream*, *Synaesthesia*, *The Nottingham Review*, *Spelk*, *Ellipsis Zine*, *Paper Swans*, *101 Words* and others. Marie is a Pushcart and The Best Short Fictions nominee and an editor of the Irish flash ezine *Splonk*.

IN THE AFTERMATH OF HURRICANE MARIA

CHRISTOPHER GONZALEZ

The other Puerto Rican from work lives alone, deep in Queens. He invites me over to watch the news coverage. We drink Bacardi neat, suck its heat through our back teeth. He worries a rosary between calloused fingers—the gesture could make this once-Catholic boy into a new Catholic man. But I remember the papery taste of Communion wafers and a mouth slick with cum; I remember false confessions, the truth a lump in my throat. He takes my hand in prayer, but Salvation isn't coming, it's passed right through us.

Christopher Gonzalez is the author of *I'm Not Hungry but I Could Eat* (SFWP 2021). His writing has appeared in *The Nation*, *Catapult*, *Atticus Review*, *The Best Small Fictions*, *Little Fiction*, and elsewhere. He is a fiction editor at *Barrelhouse* and lives in Brooklyn, NY, but mostly on Twitter @livesinpages.

FAIRY TALE IN WHICH YOU DATE THE MORALLY AMBIGUOUS BOY IN MATH

CHARLOTTE HUGHES

Shit pearls.

Go to the mind reader at the Woodlawn strip mall and pay them fifty dollars for a lesson. Plan to mind-read the boy's phone number.

You must be luminous at every social event. Take your pink plastic hand-mirror and stomp on its face; crush the mirror-shards in an apothecary bowl and swipe the powdered mirrors onto your eyelids.

All he can see is himself.

When you go to the zoo, kiss him behind the giraffe exhibit. After, when you feed the giraffes refrigerated lettuce, pretend to be shocked by their tongues that are the color of bruised feet. Feel their raised taste buds and squeal.

Debate the semantics of feminism. Tell him you believe in equality but just don't want to put yourself in a box, you know?

Cough to the rhythm of a Mozart concerto.

When he is not there at lunch, assume the role of medium. He is sitting across from you in spirit.

Go to Bi-Lo to get a brown paper bag. The night before your differential equations test, cut and paste the grocery bags into a stiff-pleated minidress.

(The next day, he will compliment you because you are not a fussy girl. You will score three points lower than him on the differential equations test because you made a silly mistake.)

When you get sick in January the only cure is twice-worn sweatshirts.

When your best friend tells you that he was messing around with a mutual friend in the parking lot, hex the mutual friend. Spiders and scorpions fall from her mouth when she speaks. She'll go to urgent care, twice.

That is the day he says he forgives you.

Piss rosewater.

Ideologically, you have already married your AmEx. You are sorry to say this to him.

The day your best friend tells you that he was messing around in the parking lot again, go to the zoo. Hex your best friend because she breathes out lies. Let the tallest giraffe lick your face with its bruised-foot tongue. It feels like a kiss.

Cry fruit-flavored vodka.

He has not texted you back for a week. Imagine that the power lines have fallen in his neighborhood, covering his house with thorns and dead signals.

That night, when you call your friends to talk and all you can hear are the sounds of spiders and scorpions crawling over the phone receivers, cry. Pour your tears in a glass and drink them all. Notice that they taste like brine.

Charlotte Hughes is a high school senior from South Carolina. Her writing can be found or is forthcoming in *West Branch*, *CutBank*, *Waxwing*, *PANK*, *Meridian*, and *Fugue*. She is the recipient of the 2020 Meridian Short Prose Prize, and a 2020 Foyle Young Poet.

OF PHOTOGRAPHY AND TRUTH

JASON JACKSON

Image

You're always embarrassed in photographs, holding up your hand, saying *wait, wait*, and it's your hair or your makeup or *there's something in my eye*, and I breathe slowly, fighting the urge to say *but you're beautiful* because you don't want to know. Later, you swipe at the screen, saying *delete, delete, delete*.

Exposure

Andrea poses for me naked in hotel bedrooms, all the lights burning and the flash bleaching her to a ghost. Her eyes hollow, and each shot is more abstract than the last. Frame after frame, I sacrifice figure and line to a magnesium absence, finding truth in the emptiness she becomes. *I'm in there somewhere*, she says, *behind all that white*.

Composition

You buy yourself a camera, take control. *I want to see why you love it so much*. You stand me in front of mountains, only ever taking one shot each time. *If it works, it works,* you say. I try to explain the rule of thirds, the leading line, but you only laugh—*you and your expertise*—and you always place the subject of the image directly in the centre of the frame. It shouldn't work, but it does: a man, a mountain, simply shown. At night, as you sleep, I go to the beach and fail to capture the ocean.

Verisimilitude

I phone because I need to see her, but her flatmate says she's gone. *You're the camera-guy, right? There's something on its way.* Two days later I come home from work to find you on the floor, surrounded. Each print is a whiteness, an indecipherable blank, but on the reverse, my scrawled messages to her, my dirty words. *Who is she?* you say, holding an image in your hand. I want to say: *can't you see she's nothing. She doesn't even exist.*

Camera Obscura

All the furniture's gone, and so are you. Faint images play against these bare walls as I take a pencil, trace the outline: the two of us, as we were. But when the sun goes down these grey scratchings will be all that's left.

Jason Jackson's fiction has appeared recently at *Fractured Lit* and *CRAFT*, as well as taking 2nd place in *The Phare's* 2021 WriteWords competition and 3rd in the 2020 *Retreat West* Short Story Competition. His prose / photography piece *The Unit* is published by A3 Press. Follow Jason on Twitter @jj_fiction

CACTUS

DI JAYAWICKREMA

The cactus is blooming, my husband says. My eyes
are shut, the insides of my eyelids are orange in
the light streaming through. I've come to believe
orange is the color of vast, unbroken love. I'm the
safest I've ever been. We live in DC, in a little house
with a patio where I sit, eyes closed, the sun warm
on my face, in a city being buried under the weight
of transplants like us. My husband strokes my arm
once before he leaves for work: a light touch to say I
needn't open my eyes. His grandmother fled Germany
just in time. I don't work this morning. During the
war in Sri Lanka, my mother went to work every
morning pretending she was taking a stroll. She
wore her everyday clothes, carrying a market bag,
slipped down a side street so an unmarked van could
ferry her to a government job always under threat of
bombing. Every night, I waited by the gate for the
van to bring her home. Years later, she would tell me
she'd never forget those rides; the smell of bodies
burning in the streets (I never asked whose bodies).
In the Negev, my husband's mother hid in a barrel

during shelling. In Sri Lanka, I practiced hiding under the desk every morning after class prayers, but the bombs never dropped on me. Now here we are. Cactus blooming, eyes closed, my husband leaving with a soft touch in the morning. We both know he'll be back in the evening. If I open my eyes, I'll think of who this city that isn't my city isn't safe for. On whose cities our mothers and our mothers' mothers built our lives, so I keep my eyes shut. This is the safety love won us.

Di Jayawickrema is a hybrid writer living in New York City. Her work has appeared in *wildness*, *Jellyfish Review*, *Pithead Chapel*, *Entropy*, and elsewhere. She is a VONA alumnus and an incoming Kundiman fellow. She is working on her first book. Visit her at dijayawickrema.com.

WHAT I'M MADE OF

RUTH JOFFRE

Paper cuts so thin and numerous they've changed my fingerprints. Jell-O thick enough that if you were to shoot arrows at my chest you wouldn't get a satisfying hit. Orgasms that have elected not to happen. Fingers that have found their way inside me anyway. Hairs that I've pulled out in rage and in lust. Other people's hair, I mean. Eyebrows and sideburns. Estrogen that's slowly leeching into me via a ring in my vagina. More eggs than I care for. More blood. More air. Assorted tubes. Various wires and sleeping pills and hospital gowns that make me wonder if I'm still human or if I have to pay the doctor's bill before I'm granted that privilege. Very little privilege. Whatever is the opposite of money— sludge, probably. Spoons made from clay instead of silver. Broken locks instead of keys. A useless piece of filigree on the jewelry box that didn't survive my move cross country. Everything I left behind, but in silhouette this time, like puppets. Like you. Your kitchen knives and your tweezers. Your name carved into my tongue so often that I say it when I breathe. Pleas. But not one ounce of forgiveness.

A GIRL OPENS A MUSEUM

RUTH JOFFRE

A Lipstick Called "Catsuit," 2019
Jet-black tube, lipstick nub, vegan

A rarity—her lips unpainted. Her favorite color wasted. In the before time, how I watched her fingertip dab dab dab the stick and swipe the color across her lips. A chocolate shell on every sentence. White cream teeth reflected in the mirror. Not a vanity—just a compact flashing for a minute between the crack and flip of an egg. Breakfast harried, dairied, full of fat and love. Imprinted on the cheek. Marked as her daughter—her blood. Mama C's chin dimpling when she finds the tube at the bottom of Mom's purse only a week after she died. I want to unremember it.

One-quarter Joy (FEMI NIST KILL JOY), 2017
Metallic pink buttons, bitter clasps, blood

Once a set. Now separated. Divided. Each bright button a pop of color in its own frame of grief. Impossible to bring them together. Unbearable to be sitting in the same room with Mama C crying. Instead, we create containers for loss: buildings

81

inside buildings, closets inside closets. I spray-paint this museum gold. Construct it out of cardboard and black electrical tape. Accent it with chevrons. Detachable roof. A hinged façade. How wrong of me to believe that pain could be elegant. It metastasizes—a tumor on her thyroid, in her throat, in her jaw. Everywhere I am she is dying. Everywhere I am she once felt joy.

Baby Blanket at Rest, 2010-2020
Hundred Acre Wood, fabric, square

No longer a source of comfort or warmth. Now a patch, a memory the size of my infant fist. Tiny screaming face in every baby picture. Soothed only by the bunch of the baby blanket around my hips. Pantsless Winnie walking through the wood in search of honey—that neverending quest. "You were always, always hungry," Mom once said, and I was always fed. Never picky except when it came time to spoon her hospital food. Cubed carrots. Meager mashed potatoes. Eventually, the feeding tube, the loss of her lullabies. Duérmete, mi niña. Duérmete, mi sol. Still half-asleep, I cut the sun out of the blanket. Mounted it on the wall. Mom.

Ruth Joffre is the author of the story collection *Night Beast*. Her work has appeared or is forthcoming in *Kenyon Review*,

Lightspeed, Gulf Coast, Prairie Schooner, The Masters Review, Hayden's Ferry Review, Pleiades, and elsewhere. She lives in Seattle, where she serves as the Prose Writer-in-Residence at Hugo House.

IT FINALLY HAPPENED

JAD JOSEY

The sun dissolved into the sea today. It finally happened this time—it was not a metaphor for your fading love or a simile about your joy winking out like a light. The sun touched down, an inverted avalanche of steam cascading skyward as our best star tipped into the ocean. I was listening to the same mockingbird we used to hear on our evening walks: he was mid-fourth call of the thirteen he sings, halfway through his trilling crescendo, when the sun extinguished for eternity. I listened to him finish in the first true darkness of my life, pulling the scarf you crocheted tight around my neck and face, yarn haunted by the ghost of your fingers. Then I leaned up against the rough bark of the mocking-bird's tree and tried to remember thirteen songs I knew before the cold swallowed us both.

Jad Josey resides on the central coast of California. His work has appeared in *Ninth Letter*, *Glimmer Train*, *Passages North*, *CutBank*, *Palooka*, and elsewhere and has been nominated for the Pushcart Prize, The Best Small Fictions, and Best of the Net. Read more at www.jadjosey.com or reach out on Twitter @jadjosey.

A LIST OF THINGS
THAT ARE WHITE

MATT KENDRICK

fluffy clouds; fluffy sheep; clowns' faces both happy and sad; the light before it spills into fickle rainbows in the water in the plastic cup on your bedside table;

your ankle socks, one rolled up, one rolled down; mist-laced memories of wellingtons pirouetting over frosty ground, hoping for snow; a polar bear called Cosmo in your mittened hand;

real-life polar bears in Svalbard, Norway; plane tickets to go there, unpurchased; the aeroplane I can see in the perplexingly cloudless sky; its vapour trail, a comet's tail; the sour cream moon I bargain with on a clear night;

in the chapel, the chaplain's cassock; her teeth, enamelled gravestones that bite words in half—she says God works in mysterious ways and fades as I leave her for downstairs disinfected corridors not flocked with sheep and clouds and clowns like the ones up here; the tissue I dab at my eyes in the lift;

then starched bedsheets tucked in at the sides; the paper on the end-of-bed clipboard with its sloppy consonants and looping vowels; the blur of the nurse as the clock mangles time into pulped-up parcels; his cheeriness as he says it's time for another round; eight little pills in a cardboard pot swallowed down with the rainbow water;

your crepe paper cheeks; the Elsa wig I bought you after we watched Frozen for the thirteenth time and you sang Let It Go's soaring chorus, determined and breathless, over and over again; your hands cold like Elsa's;

and silence and stillness

—except for the ghost that lurks in the corner of my eye; the one that has been there since you told me about the dream where everything is white; those fluttering wings of unvoiced fears; my lie that this will all be done with soon;

and in the pages of a photo album yet to be filled, an anti-ghost; you at Christmas wrinkling your nose at Brussels sprouts; you as a clown in the school play and, years later, posing with your University dissertation on Svalbard polar bears; the dress you'll wear on your wedding day; the carnation in your hair; the thought of you in your first dance as you do what you've always done and pirouette serenely through the snow.

Matt Kendrick is a writer based in the East Midlands, UK. His short fiction has appeared in the *Bath Flash Fiction Award* anthology, *CHEAP POP*, *CRAFT*, *FlashBack Fiction*, *Lunate*, *Reflex Fiction*, *Splonk* and elsewhere. He was included on the BIFFY 50 list for 2019-20.

lost daughter?

LILAC BED

TARAH KNARESBORO

We announce our desire to open for business. We are sweet and we are soft and have been told we are gorgeous. Let us make a living, flirting with tourists' ankles.

What use have you for the standard economy?

We spurn this question. We think it distasteful that it is left to those with no imagination to decide such things. We stare.

He surrenders. What do you require?

We require a sign. At the top, in bold lettering: Visit the World's Most Beautiful Lilac Patch. Underneath, smaller lettering: Two dollars. Underneath, same size: Tips welcome. Underneath, italics: *Children under 10 are asked to maintain a distance of three feet from the lilacs.*

Anything else?

That will do.

We publish your favorite authors—even the ones you haven't read yet. Get new fiction, essays, and poetry delivered to your inbox.

We begin primping. We get the xylem and phloem running up and down our stems, filling our petals with rich color. We shunt nutrients to the smallest among us. We see the groundskeeper marveling from a distance, in a posture he imagines to be subtle. We notice everything that is subtle.

Within days, we are strewn with bills and coins from the tourists. Dirt can hardly be seen. We now desire to close for business. Please remove our sign.

And of your money?

What of it? We stare. Together we hold hands for our wilting, shrinking and dulling, falling upon our bed and each other to rest, composting our bills into the soil, full as ticks stuffed with blood.

Tarah Knaresboro is a fiction writer and digital health communications designer based out of Mexico City. Her work has been published in *Electric Literature*, *The Los Angeles Review*, and *Muff Magazine*. She is working on a series of literary chatbots.

ROAD RUNNERS

KATHRYN KULPA

We made up our minds to try all the flavors of Slurpees, even the ones that sounded gross: hot blue Margarita, coffee-banana jolt. Life is boring but we're not, is what we told everybody, flashing our toe rings and our Slurpee-colored hair, and when Todd Paquette dared us to take off our tops we said we would, told him to meet us at the shut-down skate park, and flashed him our painted chests: FUCK, said yours, the U teasingly cradling your nipple; YOU, said mine, our T-shirts held to the sky across the cracked and empty cement bowl, red letters big enough for his watching friends to see. We stayed long enough to see his jaw drop, linked arms, raised middle fingers, ran home with all their too-late slams following us like wind, skanks, lezzies, hos, nothing could catch us, not even the news next morning, Todd with his father's gun, we heard that and kept running: whatever he'd tried to prove to them and failed, the crushed look in his eyes when our shirts came up, what he felt when we were gone and his friends hurled their words at him instead of us: none of it would find us if we just kept running.

Kathryn Kulpa is an editor, writing teacher, and author of a flash chapbook, *Girls on Film* (Paper Nautilus). She has stories in *Lost Balloon*, *SmokeLong Quarterly*, *Pithead Chapel*, *trampset*, *Women's Studies Quarterly*, and many other journals and anthologies.

A SHORT LIST EXPLAINING WHY I'M AN OKAY PERSON

KAT L'ESPERANCE-STOKES

Nana, my first dog. Cheerios. Hannibal, my first cat. He had two tongues and six toes on each paw. Mom painting. Mrs. Sparling, my kindergarten teacher. She's prayed. "Hannibal isn't dead he's sleeping," "No mom he's dead," Grace Chapel. Stiff pants. Collared shirts. Clean mouth. Multigrain Cheerios. Soap! Hands. Sit up. Dad's home. "He can't go into work anymore," Different books for different rooms. Adventure Zone Bible. Face cleanser. Fox News. History lectures at the kitchen / dining / homework table. Hands. First radio. History Channel. "Nothing goes on top of the Bible," "But my stuff will fall," "No it won't," "But Mrs. Wright gravity," "Nothing goes on top of the Bible." Adventure Zone Bible but with the spine cracked. His hands. Is this an okay place for hands to be? "Have you accepted God into your heart as your lord and savior?" Library books. Cool Math Games. Poptropica. He taught me how to crack my bones. Zoey 101. Soggy Cheerios. Library books overdue. Ned Declassified. Percy Jackson and the

Olympians. He taught me how to crack my knuckles. Harry Potter. Bras. "Are you sure you want to wear something that short?" "It's hot. What the worst that can happen?" His hands again. His hands again. "Oh, him? He's like a brother to me." His hands are cold. He lifted me up to teach me how to crack my spine. He lifted me up where the underwire meshed with my ribs. Is this an okay place for hands to be? He taught me how to crack my bones.

Kat L'Esperance-Stokes was born in Santa Monica during a lightning storm. After, she fell in love with folklore, horror, and the concept of home. Now you could find her in Vermont for school or on instagram and twitter @katlstokes.

A DESERT GRAVEYARD

MINYOUNG LEE

The problem with these dried-up shrubs isn't that they aren't beautiful. They are beautiful in a way that makes city people leave their manicured lawns in Beverly Hills for entire weekends to bask in this unforgiving heat and deathly cold. The problem with these dried-up shrubs is that they are stuck, because once upon a time millions of years ago, this land here was an ocean, and then it dried up over the course of those millions of years. Now all that water is gone. It's not like these shrubs could have uprooted themselves from the hundred-and-ten-degree sand and drive away in a beaten-up RV to a different patch of land with black dirt and water. They're just here and it's not their fault because it's the land that decided to turn on them. But they've always been beautiful, these shrubs. The hints of green under the dust that accumulates for months before the annual drop of rain, the fuzzy rodents they let nestle between their roots, the thorns on their branches to protect them from the men who can't help but step on them to see if they'll continue to thrive. These shrubs are beautiful. After all these years in this dear desert, she could finally see this clearly.

Minyoung Lee writes fiction and essays in Oakland, CA. Her work appears in *Monkeybicycle*, *jmww*, *trampset*, and others. Her prose chapbook *Claim Your Space* was published by Fear No Lit Press in March 2020. Her website is https://myleeis.com/.

THE GLOWING

TARA LINDIS

We were told we were part of a bright new future.
Radium was rare, sought after, the new wonder
drug. Wealthy women with completely different
lives from us clamored for radium face cream for
an infinite youthful glow. The upper classes drank
radium water and brushed with radium toothpaste.
Not all products contained the substance obviously;
not everyone could get it. But we got to work with
it, dipping our delicate brushes in the substance and
with the steadiest of hands painted the thin arms of
watches and aircraft instruments. Before, we were
ordinary, our education an indulgence. With the
boys away fighting the Great War, our incomes now
helped our families, and our work saved the lives
of pilots, possibly innocent civilians. And they said
it was safe, a harmless revolutionary new product.
And we were unique, special; we were incandescent.
We glowed like luna moths. We could see our way
home through pitch nights, led only by the magic
of our fingertips. With a brief touch, our clothes
glowed, and we were mysterious luminescent ghosts

floating down the city's streets.

Until one by one we began to disappear. Our skin sifted translucence, our bones dissolved, our teeth fell out. Each dip of the slight brush between our lips, only thirty hairs on each one, for the sliver of a minute and hour hand, and still, we died like stars, from the inside.

Tara Lindis has had work published in *Kenyon Review Online*, *The Fourth River*, *Construction Literary Magazine* and elsewhere. Originally from Portland, Oregon, she now lives in Brooklyn, New York.

FINALE

CHRISTOPHER LINFORTH

Our cellphones play an excerpt from Verdi's *Il Trovatore* in the mornings. At 6:37 we judder awake to "The Anvil Chorus," hearing the crash of hammers striking anvil faces, again and again. Our grandfather listened to this opera every Sunday instead of going to church with our parents. By the time we had picked him up for brunch, the last act blasted from the speakers in his basement. He always said the dungeon scene was his favorite, that sometimes he felt he was awaiting execution.

Our grandfather didn't die by an executioner's ax or by a guillotine blade slicing off his head—though he would have enjoyed the theatricality of both. He suffered a stroke soon after waking one Sunday morning. He lay in bed half-blind, his stunned body helpless, his semi-conscious mind unaware of the blood leaking into his skull. When we discovered his cold corpse, his eyes faced the telephone on the nightstand, the handset off the hook.

It was many years later that we realized the two of us were both using the Verdi alarm. As twins, we were not too shocked by the coincidence. For a long time growing up, we had shared a bed and woke in those early hours to the slate-blue light of daybreak. In the short time we had alone, while our parents still slept, we pressed our heads together so hard that we could feel each other's skull. Our foreheads seemed to part, frontal bones cracked open, our brains transmitting a promise that we would never die without telling the other.

Christopher Linforth is the author of three story collections, *The Distortions* (Orison Books, 2021), winner of the 2020 Orison Books Fiction Prize, *Directory* (Otis Books/Seismicity Editions, 2020), and *When You Find Us We Will Be Gone* (Lamar University Press, 2014).

WHEN ALICE BECAME THE RABBIT

CYNDI MACMILLAN

Carroll told it wrong: there was no waistcoat or pocket watch. Nobody was in a hurry or late, and my transformation had nothing to do with size. I never fell. I descended into my own realm, as weightless as a bubble. Only the wind whimpered. The truth is that I always knew who I was and who I would become. *Je suis un rêve, une reine.* In this Wonderland, the birds bestow wings. Cats still smile while riddles perk ears, but we have finally learned how to stare down the madness, freed hearts kept as bluesy companions, our life story ghosting at margins, facts burrowing under the frame of fiction.

Cyndi MacMillan's work has appeared in literary journals such as *The Dalhousie Review*, *The Ekphrastic Review*, *The Fieldstone Review*, *Freefall*, *Grain Magazine*, *Room*, *The Prairie Journal*, and *The Windsor Review*. Current works-in-progress include a mystery novel and children's first chapter books.

NEIGHBORS

ERINROSE MAGER

for Justin Phillip Reed

My neighbor harvested a solitary lemon from the potted Meyer lemon tree on his balcony. This I watched from my window. The lemon was not quite ripe; my neighbor twisted it, round and round, at the base of the stem before the fruit gave way. The Meyer tree still swayed from the harvest when my neighbor held his lemon to the light—as though to look through it or perhaps to eclipse the sun, which illuminated his balcony and cast my window in shadow. For this reason, my neighbor didn't see me—just as he hadn't seen me that entire summer while I watched his little lemon grow. I don't know: something about trying to distract myself from the other objects I owned but was still wanting of. I was living a whole life at the window, wanting of that life despite having it, and despite intuiting love in my present, my future—expecting the unknown faces of many people for whom I would soon grow deep affection. Alas, the neighbor returned inside with his lemon. Crossing the threshold, he palmed the lemon like he might an egg. It should be said, I suppose, that my neighbor's wife was dying. I'd greeted her on a few occasions by the shared dumpster, but as for this man—her husband—I never met him at all. The nurses came and went, the ambulances. I'm not sure. I'm not sure because I moved to a new city. What I mean is, I was in love, and it was time for me to feel like I was living in the buildings I was living in: a basic human right—to look around and think, Everything here could be cherished or buried or stolen, and right now it is known, I know it, and none of it is mine.

Erinrose Mager's work appears in *DIAGRAM*, *Fence*, *jubilat*, *The Adroit Journal*, and elsewhere. She lives in New York.

THE CLOWN KING

AVRA MARGARITI

The Clown King's throne is a folding chair in a
one-room apartment with a dripping faucet and
starbursts of mold crawling across the walls. Her
face is a roadmap of origami wrinkles, the laugh /
frown lines of her mouth, a balloon animal knot. The
tiny apartment can fit a troupe of forty. Clowns, as
showcased by the physics of clown cars, are known
to bend space and, occasionally, time.

The Clown King lives in a city of baguette crumbs
gobbled down by oil-slick-plumed pigeons. She
spies the geraniums on balcony flowerpots along
Main Street and thinks they look durable enough,
if a little droopy, to squirt water out of their pollen
hearts. The Clown King, ever-vigilant, rides her
velocipede around the city in order to look after her
people as they work. Lately, there have been some
coulrophobic incidents in the gray-stone streets.
They make the Clown King wary. A group of factory
workers called one of her harlequins *la féerie*, while
the mimes, in their striped uniform and tear-painted
faces, have been told repeatedly they'd look prettier
if they just smiled more.

The pierrots down by the riverfront are faring better, the Clown King is relieved to find out. They play their weeping violas and the tourists toss coins in their ripped-velvet cases. Most popular of all are the regular clowns hired for birthday parties of rosy-cheeked local children.

Life in their city of canals and towering monuments hasn't always been all fun and games, but they manage. The Clown King pedals home before her troupe arrives, bags of groceries hung from either side of the handlebars. She'll be making pies, filled with days-old cream and discount strawberries. She sits at the table and waits, a stolen flower in a tin can, pie-crust perfume covering the odor of mold.

In the evening, after her troupe of clowns and pierrots, mimes and harlequins, have broken bread around the kitchen table, the comedy and tragedy masks come off. The Clown King slips into a threadbare nightgown and washes the pancake makeup off her face.

They sleep stacked one atop the other, warm bodies a shield from the damp and cold, red noses brushing together in kaleidoscopic dreams.

A DOG LIKE A GHOST

AVRA MARGARITI

A ghost sits at the kitchen table, buttering toast. He wavers, semi-transparent. Not wanting to spook him further, I leave.

How many ghosts can fit in a house before it becomes a cemetery?

On my way to the dog shelter, I buy a deli sandwich that tastes like sawdust. Every day, I walk a different dog around the block. It gets me out of the house. Gives the ghosts some privacy, too.

"New arrival," says the shelter lady. "Poor thing. Nobody will ever want her ... too damaged."

The dog in question is dark-furred, buster-collared. A bony mixed breed. The adoption fee, less than the price of my sawdust breakfast. So I pay it.

They say depression is a black dog following you around. This dog trembles so much, she can't walk. I want to make the ones who hurt her pay, but admitting this would mean more therapy sessions. I carry the dog in my arms. The shelter lady offers me a cardboard box, but I have enough of those, unopened back at the house.

"This is your new home," I say in the entryway.

The dog's nails click against the floorboards.

It's been a while since I had company not made of ether. Months ago, the owner warned me about the "house-guests". *They're harmless*, she'd said, *a small nuisance. You won't find cheaper rent.* I'd been kicked out of my assisted-living apartment, so I thought, *I can handle the ghosts. What's some extra misery?*

When I return from the pet store hauling bags of dry food, a little girl-spirit is scratching the dog's pink belly.

"Don't stop on my account," I say, but she's already puffed out of sight.

I bathe the dog thoroughly, although I haven't washed my hair in days. Stitches peek beneath scraggly fur. She reminds me of myself, the first ghost I ever saw in the mirror.

Later, she sleeps under my bedcovers. Won't stop quivering. A rescue dog is a lot like a house ghost: skittish, whimpering, terrified of people.

What would it take to nurse her back to health? To guide my poor houseguests into the light?

I, too, am haunted by humans.

Avra Margariti is a queer Social Work undergrad from Greece. She enjoys storytelling in all its forms and writes about diverse identities and experiences. Her work has appeared or is forthcoming in *SmokeLong Quarterly*, *The Forge Literary Magazine*, *Longleaf Review*, *The Journal of Compressed Creative Arts*, and other venues.

ARMADILLO JESUS

CARSON MARKLAND

My brother was the one who found it. He's the one who'd gotten the idea that the armadillo was the second coming of Jesus Christ. He's the one who the armadillo followed around like a little brother, snuffling at his sneakers. And if you picked up Armadillo Jesus and tried to carry him away, say, to roll him down a slide at the playground, Armadillo Jesus would squeal like a pig until he was in my brother's arms again. So we were all a little disappointed when somebody's dog got a hold of it and more or less tore it to shreds. It seemed like if it really was Jesus Christ, crucifixion was bad enough the first time around, much less getting chewed to death by a golden retriever.

We'd taken to feeding it, dressing it up. It liked Cheetos; oatmeal crème pies not so much. We made it a pope hat out of a napkin and some tin foil. We pushed it around in somebody's old yellow baby stroller and told the little kids that if they gave us money, Armadillo Jesus would send them straight to Heaven. We racked up a pretty good profit from that and splurged on Blue Raspberry Icees from the 7-Eleven, but then somebody started to feel bad, so we shared with the little kids too, letting their mouths turn blue, listening to them shriek about brain freeze.

But then: golden retriever. Dead armadillo.

When we first found Armadillo Jesus, gutshot and leaking innards, I thought that was that. Party's over. The other kids, they sort of wandered off, talking about how maybe they'd go throw rocks at the mail truck now to entertain themselves. But my brother—he scooped up Armadillo Jesus, held him like a baby, stained his gray sweatshirt with blood even though our mom pitches a fit when we get blood on our clothes because it's the hardest to wash out.

We built Armadillo Jesus a tomb in the woods. Well, really it was just a cardboard box. But we put Armadillo Jesus inside, and my brother closed the flaps and sealed it with tape and said, "Three days," and wouldn't come home with me for dinner and when my mom asked, "Where's your brother?" I said "Waiting."

Carson Markland is a writer and filmmaker from South Carolina. She studied English and Creative Writing at Wake Forest University, where she was the recipient of the DA Brown Award in Creative Writing. Her work has appeared in SmokeLong Quarterly and Laurel Moon.

THREE POSTCARDS

KATHLEEN MCGOOKEY

–from Bellingrath Gardens

Dear Mother, Edith got hold of a horoscope—
our guide distributed them, to shake things up—
and now there is no stopping her. Never mind the
lovely stone steps curving through cascades of flame
azaleas, never mind the ivy scaling the cypress,
never mind the mermaid fountain quietly splashing
in its calm little pool. Now Edith is a bit too inter-
ested in her lucky number, counting the mourning
doves in the cedar, the pennies handed back to her
(noting whether bright or dull), each fallen lily
along our path. She feels soon she will have absolute
proof—and I disagree—that "important people are
watching" and "unexpected directions could reveal
hidden treasure." Even our stoic bus driver raised
his eyebrows after she gave him a crumpled camellia
she pulled from her purse.

–from Rochester Memorial Hospital

Dear Mother, Edith does not want me to say
exactly what happened. As usual, she has put me in a
difficult position. Witnesses agreed our guide acted

heroically. There was little blood and no permanent stains. While our stay here is considered a precaution, Edith is determined to miss nothing: she made the nurses reposition her bed toward the window. (It overlooks the parking lot.) You will receive reimbursement for the three days of touring we have missed. We are receiving excellent care, though the nurses' attention borders on fanatical. Already today one has changed my sheets, washed my hair, and delivered a small bouquet of violets. They bring us menus three times a day and though the choice is limited, we are allowed to select what most pleases us. Edith has grown partial to the tapioca pudding, which arrives in a glass like a little parfait.

–from the Place du Palais, Monaco

Dear Mother, today was an overturned rowboat, purposely left on shore. Today was a blister on my big toe. Today was a dropped coin that rolled between the table and the wall at the cafe, out of reach. Today was the skinny stray cat, limping, with mottled fur and dull eyes, that we both pretended to ignore. Edith was the sudden downpour and I had no umbrella. I was the cloudless sky afterward, washed clean.

Kathleen McGookey's most recent books are *Instructions for My Imposter* (Press 53) and *Nineteen Letters* (BatCat Press). Her work has recently appeared in *Copper Nickel*, *Crazyhorse*, *December*, *Field*, *Glassworks*, *Miramar*, *Quiddity*, and *Sweet*. She lives in Middleville, Michigan with her family.

THE RINGMASTER'S BOYS

FRANKIE MCMILLAN

Circus closed because the war was on but you wouldn't know it, we was all so alive on the inside, cartwheeling over the railway bridge and when the sleepers started shuddering under our feet we knowed it was the night train's coming, watched it sweep around the bend, horn blasting, lights flashing and us half-blinded and jumping *now!* into the dark water below, bobbing up and down like candy apples, yelling out to each other "You there Sugar, you there, Mule, you there Joey boy?" and later slipping and clawing our way up the mud bank, running back to the bunkhouse through the forest, coming out taller than the trees, we were highflyers, we'd beat that train, we was magnificent and hurry now, wet clothes over the guy ropes, snatching a look at Joey boy, naked as a horse and already seeing the map of our own lives and not knowing if it was good or half-good or otherwise but laughing anyway and later much later when we saw smoke and heard the guns we told ourselves we'd beat the train, and when the trees in the forest caught alight and the burning turned the sky red, we said we jumped the bridge and later again when black soot fell and our faces looked like cooked apples and we were hopping around in the heat we told ourselves, no matter, everyone gets saved in the circus.

Frankie McMillan is the author of five books, the most recent of which, *The Father of Octopus Wrestling and other small fictions*, was listed by Spinoff as one of the 10 best New Zealand fiction books of 2019. She has won numerous awards and creative writing residencies including the NZSA Peter and Dianne Beatson Fellowship, 2019.

ORNITHOLOGIA CORVIDAE

SARAH MCPHERSON

A Murder of Crows

The day I met him, the ornithologist told me corvids were the most intelligent birds. He kept telling that joke: attempted murder. I asked him if they used knives.

A Clattering of Jackdaws

I keep a jar of change—like my gran—for emergencies, though she raided it for cribbage night. His disapproval hovered, beady-eyed, when I picked pennies in the street.

A Band of Jays

He wanted me in fine feathers. I became talented at mimicry, playing a part, vibrant in blue—his favourite colour—my voice indistinguishable from his song.

An Unkindness of Ravens

It bothered him that I favoured myth over science. Thoughts and memories can be cruel, but I was happy, I suppose, before their dusk-shadowed wings swept between us.

A Charm of Magpies

The day I left, I caught my image looking out from the mirror and knew her, finally; sorrow and joy writ in monochrome, secrets safe behind sharp eyes.

Sarah McPherson is a Sheffield-based writer and poet, with work published in *Ellipsis Zine*, *Splonk*, *STORGY Magazine*, *The Cabinet of Heed*, and elsewhere. She has been long / short-listed in competitions including *Writers' HQ*, *Reflex Fiction* and *Cranked Anvil*. She tweets as @summer_moth and blogs at https://theleadedwindow.blogspot.com/.

GOOD STRETCH

REBECCA MEACHAM

My neighbors have always been little old men. I watch them from my bedroom window. They putter in their gardens with their broad straw hats and hang their wives' plus-sized panties on the line, self-conscious about their womanish ways in full view of, let's be honest, a hot young thing like me. I'm a two-time Fitness Olympics Regionals champ. Each dawn I run a quick 15 K and I feel their eyes, the clouded eyes of little old men, early risers, sitting on their porches in the graying mists, parade-waving and nodding hello, admiring my sculpted abs and my firm, full breasts in my pink sports bra and my swishing, silky skort.

I allow some jiggle in the right places. I do this just for them. I warm the pockets of little old men. I thread their thumb-worn inseams. What else is in their day? They watch me in my driveway, cooling down, bending low to touch my trainers, fingering my dew-slick laces, pushing my glutes up to the sky, my signature moonrise.

Inside the houses of little old men, their wives

grease skillets with bacon fat and slice daybreak into wedges of honeydew, yelling tasks from smoky kitchens, they won't even poke their curlers out.

So I make it a good stretch. I feel the burn.

Later, at my bedroom window I am back-lit, nude. I glisten. Night coughs through the yawning bedrooms of little old men, poor guys, and so, for them, I reach. I release. Let the yap-dogs rattle their chain-link fences. Let the hand-hemmed curtains part and close, part and close. My heat seeps into their faded coverlets and soaks their whiskered chins until I glow in the bones of those little old men like radium.

Rebecca Meacham is the author of two award-winning fiction collections. Her flash prose has been scored into music, translated into Polish, and carved into woodblock then letter-pressed by steamroller. A professor at UW-Green Bay, Rebecca directs the Writing and Applied Arts BFA program. Someday, she'll finish her novel.

MAGIC BULLET

BILL MERKLEE

Nobody buys the bullshit of the magic bullet that tore through JFK and Governor Connally in 1963, but I'm telling you there are magic bullets in the world, at least as far back as 1896 when my grandfather is six years old running around one of the nicer houses in Dumont, New Jersey, with his little brother Harry, where he finds his father's pistol under a pillow, his small hands struggling with the weight of it as he aims at his brother (because that's what boys do—we all had guns and tried to outdo each other with our death throes), where the gun goes off and that bullet makes Harry three years old forever, makes their parents' marriage disappear, turns my grandfather's liver to stone, explodes his marriage into porcelain shards and broken faith, ricochets through his war-weary sons, lays him in an unmarked grave in Brooklyn, and finds me bullet-proof before my children.

Bill Merklee loves short stories, short films, and short songs. His work has appeared in *CHEAP POP*, *Cabinet of Heed*, *Ellipsis*

Zine, Bending Genres, X-R-A-Y Literary Magazine, Ghost Parachute, Gravel, and *Columbia Journal* among others. Find him at billmerklee.com and on Twitter @bmerklee. He lives in New Jersey.

ARRHYTHMIA

SHAREEN K. MURAYAMA

Imagine a line between the nipples. Put your hands on the center of the chest right below that line. No, you don't have to remove the bra. This is the scene I imagine will break my Adam. Splayed out on the promenade, I heed to their heel, covered by other demands, to stop real pain: when life outlives your life-long partner.

Internally, I forget to count the dark: your last birthday, the two-hand count before retiring, and the year after? I'll be all the numbers greater than the sighs in your ballads. Meanwhile, I'm crumpling a tinge of blue, like showcase lights in front of Nordstrom's Rack, worrying about oxygen, a thing I can't see. I'm lying to myself on the sidewalk of passerbyers and weddings, thinking jellyfish have no brains and no hearts. Some of us are spared questioning what's fueling through our limbs. Some of us drift and settle for the ocean floor.

When my dad was in the care home, he needed help with his advance health directives. *Would you want CPR or other resuscitation if your heart were to stop beating?* It's an uncontrollable sound, like crying, that rises and falls with each birthday and holiday card. Each song floods the banks and rivers. *Do you want to donate your eyes?*

After my father's and husband's deaths, I wintered on writing; I panted through pain. When my waters broke, they husband-stitched my fingertips after pushing out what couldn't be said: thirty compressions and a few rescue breaths, my body spoons over a reef. How can you see what doesn't belong to you anymore?

I think my heart may have turned on me with little fists, when my dad said, *Try. At least once.*

Shareen K. Murayama is a Japanese American and Okinawan American poet and educator. She has degrees from OSU-Cascades and the University of Hawai`i at Manoa. She's a reader for *The Adroit Journal* and has pieces published or forthcoming in *The Margins, Juked, Bamboo Ridge, Puerto del Sol,* and elsewhere.

Atlas and Alice
Literary Magazine

TONIGHT

HEMA NATARAJU

One of two things can happen tomorrow:

either the parents will accept their newborn the way he is, despite the beard that touches the tips of his toes, wrap him in a thick blanket to hide his luminous face—which will glow brighter in the inky darkness of the night as they whisk him home through the hospital back door and then contemplate moving far, far away; to a place where nobody can follow and make a lab rat or a messiah of their sweet child.

Or

the mother will cry soft sobs saying over and over again that this is for the best. While the father, holding a dam of tears behind his icy exterior, abandons the baby by the dumpster behind the hospital, the mother will get on her knees, swallow the pain of fresh taut stitches tugging at her belly and pray that the world doesn't make a lab rat or a messiah of her sweet child.

But tonight,

the baby is nestled between the soft pillows of his mother's arms. She kisses his forehead and strokes his beard, while his father wipes away an errant happy tear. Outside, hospital security guards struggle to keep the crowd trying to catch a glimpse of the miraculous, freakish baby under control. Nurses sift through offerings that desperate people leave at the hospital door; keep the good stuff for themselves. One has her hand in her pocket, her fist guarding a lock of the baby's beard which she cut off while bathing him and tonight, she is sure her husband's cancer will be cured.

Tonight,

the baby's velvety beard glows golden and fiery, like a flashlight during a power cut as he feeds at his mother's breast. He smells like her childhood, like effervescent giggles with her friends, like guava slices with salt and chili, her safe, obedient childhood in which she never cheated in hopscotch games, never stole tamarind pods from the neighbor's tree like her friends did and little secrets that she never spilled and held close to her heart because she had pinky-promised.

Tonight,

cocooned in the tight space between his mother's arms, the bearded infant dreams of a sky studded with baby diamonds, growing slowly and hardening, hardening like his mother's resolve.

Hema Nataraju is a Singapore-based writer and mom of two. Her work has appeared in *Atlas & Alice Literary Magazine*, *Ellipsis Zine*, *MORIA*, *Sunlight Press*, and in print anthologies including *Bath Flash Fiction Award* 2020, *Best Microfiction* 2020, and *National Flash Fiction Day*. She tweets about her writing and parenting adventures as m_ixedbag.

HEMIBOREAL

ELSA NEKOLA

At that time we were living in a hemiboreal region, dying to be warm. The summers were short and cool, the lilacs didn't bloom until June, and somewhere across the vast glacial lake was Canada. Over the six-month winter we went to my uncle Paivo's house way out in the pine woods and shut ourselves in the sauna, tapped each other's naked backs with birch twigs, and giggled, because there wasn't much else to laugh about. Then Paivo gave us hot coffee in mugs with the handles broken off, and we sat in his tiny kitchen that smelled of venison jerky and burned wood, sweating under our burdensome clothes. This was in the Upper Peninsula of Michigan, a few years ago, when we were still married and talking about getting a dog, learning to downhill ski. At night we curled together on a futon on the floor, legs inter-twined, not out of desire but for body heat. I think the weather saved us; for a while there was always something to talk about: the dramatic November storms, the lake-effect snow, our dried-out skin, and the way our lungs prickled every time we went outside and drew a breath. I came to fear the thaw, when those conversations, those unanimous complaints, would end.

With the changing season, you saw our marriage for what it was: a slapped-together thing, a blight-stricken limb. The lake warmed up to fifty degrees, and I waded to my knees in shallow, iron-tinged water, squinting at distant ore boats, wondering where we'd gone. In summer, when you weren't cutting down trees and I wasn't waiting tables, we lay on our lawn like cats in the sun, purring, smiling, speechless. I knew it was over, but the days were longer, stretched out so far sometimes we couldn't see the other side. You live in South Carolina now, where these real-izations come easy to you. I'm still up here, sitting in the sauna alone while Paivo brushes snow off my car. I don't wait for spring anymore; I let the days go by, comforted by the slow passage of time, the relentlessness of winter, this place's commitment to it. I don't take anything for granted.

Elsa Nekola's fiction has appeared in Ploughshares, Nimrod, Witness, and other journals. Her short story collection, Sustainable Living, won the 2020 Spokane Prize for Short Fiction and is forthcoming from Willow Springs Books. She lives in Madison, Wisconsin.

STRANGER DISCONNECTED

DARREN NUZZO

The banner atop the webpage says you'll be paired with seven F's for every two M's—that's how they get you. The ratio is actually much different. I've only seen one F. She was thirteen and from the Philippines. I asked her *Buttigieg or Biden* and she thought I was talking about laundry detergent. When she lived in Quezon City, her family used Ariel. In Manila, they switched to Zonrox. Then the conversation moved to dish soap until we ran out of opinions on the matter. That was my one experience with an F. Mostly, it goes like this: *M 22, M 27, Stranger disconnected*. It's a good idea for a website, linking one stranger to another. It's just that the math doesn't add up. M's want F's and F's are smarter than that. For me, I just want someone to talk to. So I've changed letters, fixed the problem for most everyone. Things have been going much better ever since. Are you tall? is one of my favorite things to ask. You sound tall, I like to assure them. That always makes the M feel big and strong, and I know that's important. I like to ask what they do for work. If M says he does construction, I say, "Like an architect." If M says he hasn't read a book in eleven years, I say, "There's nothing found between pages a smart guy like you can't find on Earth." When M says he has insomnia, I say, "The brightest minds always do." And when M tells me all the good things about his penis, I let him know that I really believe him. They never want me to leave. But I say goodnight and move to the next, well aware of this unique opportunity I've been given, the chance to put the most good into the world at the cost of the least evil, (sinning) to the smallest degree possible, telling man everything he needs to hear, lying by just a single letter.

WOW. Stinks a+ to me?

Darren Nuzzo is the author of *I'll Give you a Dollar if you Consider this Art* and (forthcoming) *Cover Your Ears, I Have Something to Say.* He is 28.

Guy decides to go into chat rooms as a girl and uses it to hype up lonely men. Really beautiful.

REHEARSAL

NUALA O'CONNOR

Marty's car was a hearse, so that was the first turn on. Then there were his maroon lips, so girlish, so startling against his waxy skin.

Mother was appalled, of course. "He's three times your age," she said.

"Get knotted," I said, and drove around with Marty in that Cadillac with its curtained windows where the dead used to lie.

At night, we parked behind Tesco and, in the coffin space, Marty peeled off my fishnets, restricto-knicks, and double F bra. And with those wine-bright lips he drank me down, plundered from every inch of me, while I lay under him, thinking of soil.

She horny.

Nuala O'Connor lives in Galway, Ireland. *NORA*, her novel about Nora Barnacle, wife and muse to James Joyce, appeared 2021 in the USA, Ireland and Germany. Her chapbook of historical flash, *Birdie*, was recently published by Arlen House. Nuala is editor at flash e-zine *Splonk*. www.nualaoconnor.com

Girl dates older guy. he's weird. Mom doesn't approve. They FUCK.

RED

MELISSA OSTROM

Should she have ignored him? He smiled. Should she not have smiled back? He asked her where her friends were. Should she have lied? Should she have said somewhere around here, somewhere nearby? Should she not have been alone in the first place? Was a girl allowed to walk in these woods alone? He said he liked her outfit. She said thank you. Should she not have worn this outfit? Not have worn red? When he asked her where she was going, should she have said to visit her boyfriend the cop, her father the pastor, her grandfather the judge? And when she opened the door to the house in the woods, should she have locked it behind her? Should she have realized a lock would make no difference? That safety, happiness, and hope were already gone? Should she have noticed the fruit flies over the bowl of Winesaps, how the flies weren't burrowing but hovering, disturbed, and traveling fast? And what about her grandmother? When Grandma didn't answer her hello, should she have left? Should she have grabbed the poker by the hearth, just in case? Should she have cleared her throat and prepared to scream, ~~new~~ just in case? Should she have shouted out the window for help, for an eyewitness, for someone to believe her, just in case? Like the hunter she saw in the hunting blind by the stream. Would he hear her? Would he help her? Would he hurt her, too? And what about the stranger? Should she confront him? Fight him? Try to escape him? Would she stand a chance? Would she even see him coming? Would she notice his shadow in the uncertain, soft light that pooled across the floor?

Ooh damn.

Melissa Ostrom is the author of *The Beloved Wild* and *Unleaving*. Her stories have appeared in many journals and been selected for *The Best Small Fictions* 2019 and *Best Microfiction* 2020. She teaches English at Genesee Community College in western New York. Learn more at www.melissaostrom.com or find her on Twitter @melostrom.

Girl is raped(?) by guy she meets in bar. Author uses Little Red Riding Hood as a basic road map for the story.

AUTOPSY REPORT

ABIGAIL OSWALD

What I know: That after you died they opened your body like an envelope to let your secrets spill out of you. That the scalpel was stainless steel and reflective in fluorescent light. That they searched your insides as if any kind of truth could be found within your small intestine, your spleen, your lungs. That your heart weighed seven ounces when a stranger held it in her hands. That this is small for a woman's heart. That it did not beat when she held it. That it last beat on Tuesday night, only hours after you left the restaurant where you worked. That no oxygen moved through your airways for approximately eight minutes. That eight minutes was all it took. That before they weighed you in pieces, they catalogued your bruises and your scars. That the medical examiner discovered a small white cut healed over between your index and middle fingers, which I had never seen. That there are many small accidents which could leave this kind of mark. That you had scars you'd never mentioned to me, which were your secrets alone, even though they existed outside of you. That secrets do not appear

[handwritten annotations: "Key Line" with underline under "only hours after you left the restaurant where you worked"; "W geon't" next to "after you left the restaurant"; underline under "which I had never seen"]

written on the lobes of the brain when a stranger holds it in her hands.] That they sewed you back up with synthetic thread, an approximation of a whole human form, so I could look at you one last time. That all I could remember in that moment was how I'd made you years ago inside of me. That you were four pounds, six ounces, a small thing, the weight of many hearts. That this made you a probability, but never a guarantee.

I thought it was a wife!

Abigail Oswald is a writer whose work predominantly examines themes of celebrity, crime, and girlhood. She holds an MFA from Sarah Lawrence College and resides in Connecticut. Her writing has appeared in *Wigleaf*, *matchbook*, *Hobart*, *Split Lip*, and elsewhere. Find her online at abigailwashere.com.

Woman tells us what the doctors have told her regarding the autopsy of her DAUGHTER. She tells us facts I believe to give the author psychic Distance.

AN ESSAY ABOUT GHOSTS

LEE PATTERSON

in this essay you are a ghost & I am in the kitchen, boiling a pot of water. I look out my kitchen window & watch a ladder fall from the sky. it lands directly into the middle of my backyard. your ghost doesn't climb down the ladder. instead, your ghost parachutes out of a cloud in the shape of a cloud. these days I am finding it difficult to not find things difficult. I fear the mundane like you used to fear spiders, snakes, dark alleys, losing your car keys, & affording your insurance deductible. *do ghosts need health insurance?* I ask your ghost. your ghost shakes her head as steam rises from the kettle on the stove. I pour a cup of chamomile tea & think about looking out the kitchen window. instead, I pour the tea down the sink & go back to bed.

Lee Patterson's poetry has appeared in *Hobart*, *Roanoke Review*, *Ethel Zine*, *Thin Air Magazine*, and *Milk Candy Review*, among others.

THERE'S A TRICK WITH A KNIFE

MEGHAN PHILLIPS

The knife thrower picks her volunteers based on how they'll look with their backs against her fake wall, their wrists restrained in little Velcro loops. How the man in the striped T-shirt will look with an apple on his head. How the girl in the sundress will look with a balloon in either hand. Their lips softened to a surprised "o." A perfect little gasp when the apple slices, when the balloon pops.

She picks her volunteers based on how they'll look tumbled in her floral sheets. How they'll fill up her trailer at the night end of the midway. Mouths wrapped in a surprised "o" as she drags a tooth down their neck, drags a nail down their thigh. A perfect little gasp as she thinks: *what if I slip just this once.*

Meghan Phillips is the author of the chapbook *Abstinence Only* (Barrelhouse), and her stories have appeared most recently in *Okay Donkey*, *Hayden's Ferry Review*, and *Fractured Lit*. She was a 2020 National Endowment for the Arts literature fellow. To find out more about Meghan and her writing visit meghanphillips.com.

THE BOOK OF WHAT IF

PATRICK PINK

In Pio's backpack was a slice of cold pepperoni pizza
from last night, two Gala apples that still kept their
crunch, an eco-bottle of water he refilled in the Z
station's toilet, an extra pair of undies which passed
the sniff test and the Book of What If his nan gave
him when he turned thirteen. He took to the road
when the moon was a thin bowl of darkness, a cup
of possibility, Okoro. Blood stirred like rapids. Feet
were impatient and eager.

Em came upon him during their dusk run and
asked Pio where he was heading with such stride
and determination. Pio told them he was filling
out his part of the Book of What If and needed to
make the far riverbend by dawn when the taniwha,
basking in the sliver of moonlight, would finish
its dark song. Is there room enough for me in your
book, Em said because they secretly liked Pio and
Pio secretly liked them so he smiled but quickly
acted tough but Em saw through it, punched Pio
in the shoulder and together, munching Galas and
passing the Z water, they walked the loose metal

into the far hills.

The riverbend was just a riverbend. The taniwha was nowhere to be seen. Its song didn't strum the air. All hope and magic were vanishing night. Nan still had cancer. Pio still was scared. Em held his hand while Pio fingermarked his unwritten page and felt the weight of what if.

Patrick Pink lived significant amounts of his life in Michigan, Texas and Germany before settling in Aotearoa, New Zealand. His short fiction has been published in international anthologies and on-line journals. His work has been illustrated and read on the radio. He is an avid flash fiction fan.

STELLA IS

CLAIRE POLDERS

Stella is eight. She rubs a bowl between her legs, enjoying the smooth sweetness, until her mother snatches it away and tells her to behave. Stella is fourteen. Her mouth is too hungry for words when she presses her hips against his. Stella is eighty-seven. She lays her soft hand against his stubbled cheek and tells him it's OK to let go. Stella is twenty. In control. She moans, teetering on the edge of coming and building his excitement, until she rides out the crest of pleasure for them both. Stella is thirty-three. Her breasts are as round as her belly, as he soap-massages her in the bath from clavicles to toes. Stella is sixteen. She guides his hand toward her vulva, whispering about the forbidden bowl. But, no, she's not yet ready to meet that other part of him there. Stella is fifty-two. On a skin-thin moment of delight, her nipples swell like buds in spring. The scent of sex grows on his chest all day. Stella is thirty-nine. She pushes the twins on their garden twin swing. Stella is sixty-four. Retired, she gets a pilot's license and takes him up in the air so they can revel in weightlessness. Stella is seventeen. He watches her parents bury her body—a free fall down a cliff—in the dress he bought for the night they'd planned to share their first time.

NOOOOOOO

Claire Polders is a Dutch author of five novels. Her latest, *A Whale in Paris*, (Atheneum, Simon & Schuster, 2018) is a historical novel for younger readers. Her short fiction and nonfiction has been published, among others, in *Prairie Schooner*, *Tin House*, *Electric Literature*, and *Denver Quarterly*.

MOON WATCHING

REGAN PUCKETT

The astronaut is napping in his spaceship. It isn't really a spaceship, not yet, with its sharp edges and weak base, pieces of scrap metal pasted together like an elementary school art project, but one day, it will be. His wife let him keep it in the garage for a while, back when the structure was a mere sketch hanging on the wall and a pile of bolts on his desk, but it grew too real and she made him move it to the backyard.

What will the neighbors think? he'd asked, nerves blossoming in his stomach. She'd smiled, shook her head as she yanked her sleeves above her elbows, and began to carry it outside.

I'm going to take you to space one day, he promised. *We'll waltz on Venus and drink tea on Mars.*

She stared at the hunks of junk in a way that made him think she believed him, in a way that made him want to believe in himself, too.

Now, he's fallen asleep inside of his someday ship with a rusted wrench tucked in his fingers, with dreams of faraway galaxies and cherry pie.

The dying sun rays lick his skin as the hot August afternoon melts into a breezy evening. Soon enough, the stars will emerge, and his wife will crawl into the spaceship beside him. He'll trace the constellations of freckles that spot her arms as she folds her body into his. And when the cicadas begin to sing, they'll watch the moon bloom through the metal slots above their heads, dream of what it will one day feel like to watch the earth instead.

Regan Puckett lives in the Ozarks, where she writes tiny stories and drinks big cups of coffee. Find her recent work in *MoonPark Review*, *trampset*, and more.

STREETS

XOŞMAN QADO

*translated from the Kurmanji by Zêdan Xelef
and David Shook*

On our street, the moon forgot its leg—no one
trips over it. In the middle of the night, only the
dogs tear into it, but none is happy with their ration,
their hungry eyes insatiable. And so their barking is
extinguished by the crinkling of plastic bags. Dogs'
barking does not annoy me; perhaps it is the only
indisputable perception, especially when the power
cuts out at this time of night.

No one trusts the city streets any longer, and the
streets trust no one either. The buildings, too, tip
their gutters to pour their algae onto mute life. The
gutters are mysteries of thirst, and so the roofs drive
the water into them.

Outside every house, there is a diminutive dream
that complains about the high walls that surround
it. Only the windows smile at the sparrows, the
only ones who can reach them. The neighborhood
children lay the rubble they've made of the walls on
the street like a rug. Children turn everything into

143

games and then forget to play them. The streets, too, break the children's hearts with their emptiness— only dogs lie in their arms. Children and streets are both twins and enemies at the same time, neither sufficient for the other's dreams. Only abandonment changes minds and stokes the waves of forgetting. In children's minds, time too pampers itself like a bride, becomes a candy to be enjoyed on the feast day.

Xoşman Qado is a poet, translator and editor in Rojava, the de facto autonomous region of northeastern Syria.

David Shook is a poet and translator in Marshall, CA.

Zêdan Xelef is a poet, translator, and MFA student at San Francisco State University.

CITY OF SERENA

DAWN RAFFEL

In the beautiful city of Serena, every old woman wears a mask. The body may yet appear lithe in slacks, in silks, in exquisitely calculated jackets; the gait still steady in the cleverest shoes. The hair is calibrated to perfection, dyed, snipped. And yet the face—the face!—cannot be made to please the eye, by needle, by knife, emollient, unguent, pressure, laser, poison, paint. And so the old women of Serena go about in vivid masks: the poor in the primary colors; the wealthy in the jewel tones, garnet and sapphire, emerald, all of it fired in the city's famous ovens. Time was, the old women removed their masks at night, in the dark, but now it is the law that they must wear them, even to sleep, even to die. The hands must be gloved. The toes must be sheathed. The old women of Serena may be sixty or ninety, or two-hundred and ten. Despite their wild hues, no one sees them at all.

GORGEOUS

Dawn Raffel is the author of five books, most recently *The Strange Case of Dr. Couney.*

SOME ROSES ONLY NEED PEPSI

ANGELA READMAN

Dad scrabbles on his knees wrestling thorns. His arms look freckled, but close-up, anyone could see the freckles are blood. I don't get that close. I hug the swear jar while he battles the roses that keep coming back.

The petals are smoky. Since they widened the road, they stink of petrol and the buds shrivel like lips shrinking what they're dying to say a bit more every day.

Bleach hasn't worked, pruning, not even cat shit. We don't water the flowers, they don't care. Lorries fly by, drivers fling bottles of piss out the window and they suck up the dregs of painkillers and Pepsi.

The last time I picked a rose, I'd been out with Mom to a Damaged Tock Sale. The poster said Purses, Designer, Bargains, but underneath it said *Damaged Tock*. Mom took me to the warehouse that couldn't spell like someone fixing a broken clock.

The purses were leather. Sequin, velvet, you name it. I even saw one made of juice pouches. The oranges looked smoggy. Everything was furry with dust or had wonky stitches, but the purses were still beautiful. Mom said. She sniffed the leather, hugging two, struggling to decide between crocodile or snakeskin. The guy said she could have both. Pretty lady, like you, he said, what the hell.

She walked out swinging the purses so high a campervan beeped its horn. When we came home, she kept putting different stuff inside the purses. Cigarettes and coupons. No, lipstick and cigarettes. Lipstick, a tampon, a notebook and pen. All night, she got up during *The Masked Singer* just changing bits. Like the satin lining didn't suit everything and the purses had to try on what fit.

Lady, she said, lady.

The sun makes Dad's neck jerky, a lorry zooms by and he hurls the flying bottle over the fence. I bundle branches in my arms and carry them to the firepit. Even snipped the rosebuds lilt towards the light, desperate as a woman craning for someone to really look her in the eye.

mom is the roses + rose bud

Angela Readman's story collection *Don't Try This at Home* won The Rubery Book Award. Her stories have won the Costa Short Story Award, the Mslexia and The Anton Chekhov Award for Short Fiction. Her poetry, *The Book of Tides*, is published with Nine Arches. Her debut novel is *Something like Breathing* (2019.)

MYTH BITCH

NO'U REVILLA

Before we stopped speaking, my mother told me of an all-woman island. *My side of the family*, she said, her mouth twisting like a sick branch. *And the women are witches.* I have since dreamed of women with heads of barbed wire. Torso in the bedroom, breasts in the sink. Legs divided between O'ahu and Maui. Is *witch* the right word? When I sleep with a new woman, my mother whispers *fetus* into her fingers and sews my mouth shut. The fetus of a witch becomes a bitch. No daughter of hers will sleep like that. For the self-segmenting woman armed with needle and thread, rhyme is a mnemonic device. Repetition is rope. I will always look like her. Repeat: say nothing, daughter. Repeat: sleep alone, daughter. Daughter the word for *stitch her close*. When my blood touches her blood it means my mother spits needles. When I dream of women and wire it means I fuck like a woman at war with her body. Where is my rope? I am a witch. Or I am an island. Or am I a love story misinterpreted? Fetus eating with a face to memorize. Mother, I am the myth bitch you dream about.

No'u Revilla is a queer Native Hawaiian writer, educator, and aloha 'āina. She taught poetry at Pu'uhuluhulu University in the summer 2019 and is an Assistant Professor at the University of Hawai'i-Mānoa, where she teaches creative writing, decolonial poetics, and Native Hawaiian Literature.

conflict—ship run aground

FOUNDERING

MATTHEW J. RICHARDSON

It's only when Ma and Pa wake me that I realise the cries weren't in my dreams. I'm told to get dressed quickly. Truth be told there's not much to put on—a shirt and the only pair of breeches that I own. I dress and sit on my bed, rubbing the sleep out of my eyes and watching the cruisie lamp throwing its flickering light against the stone walls.

Ma comes for me soon enough, her face grim. We're out of our longhouse and walking up to the cliffs before I've finished yawning. Pa is up ahead, his lantern swinging a pool of light ahead and behind him. Soon it joins a dozen others, all of them bobbing in the hands of grim-faced crofters. Ma, my sister and I hurry to keep up.

The screams are louder now and as we crest the cliffs we see her. The ship is exactly where I knew she'd be, at a strange angle against the rocks, a collier by the look of her. She's heaving in the swell. I can hear the deck planks groaning, and through the rain and the sea spray I can see small figures clinging to the rigging and to the masts.

It's cold. I try to snatch the shawl that my sister has thought to bring out with her. Ma stops me and we all turn back to watch the ship. There's nothing we can do. That fact doesn't stop us looking, though. The whole village comes up when there's a ship run aground. It's not something that we enjoy, exactly. Pa says that we've got a duty to go, that if our lanterns on the cliffs give those sailors some small measure of comfort we'll have done our bit.

There's tales from the folk up the coast. Stories that we stand by as men drown. Mutterings that sailors are thrown back into the sea after clambering onto the rocks. I don't know anything about that. What I do know is that it'll be light in a few hours. It's only a collier, sure, but it's not every day a ship founders, even on this headland. There'll be rich pickings in the shallows.

[handwritten: IDK what to think.]

Matthew is a public sector worker and doctoral student. He has stories in publications including *Gold Dust magazine*, *Literally Stories*, *Close to the Bone*, *McStorytellers*, *Fiction Junkies*, *Soft Cartel*, *Whatever Keeps the Lights On*, *FlashBack Fiction*, *CafeLit*, and *Shooter*. Matthew tweets at @mjrichardso0 and blogs at www.matthewjrichardson.com.

VELCRO SHOES

SONIA ALEJANDRA RODRÍGUEZ

At nine—I can't stop the trips and falls, the scrapes of my knees against concrete. I like the burn and the drum of my blood gushing out of me. I am split skin. My father teaches me to tie my shoes. Because he's tired of watching me fall. Or, because he's tired of picking me up. Hands me the left shoe: "Do as I do?" he says, using the right shoe as an example. And I do what he does—until my mid-twenties, when I've pushed everyone I love away, too. He forms two loops with each of the laces, crosses them, pushes one through the opening, pulls tight. "Only one can go through. The other can't. Entiendes?" And I didn't know then it was our farewell. I get good at making it seem like my shoes are tied—I tuck the laces into the bottom of my shoes, into my socks, press on the aglets with my heels. I fall and I am split skin and gushing blood. My mother gets me a new pair of Velcro shoes "para que no batalles," she says. That's what my mother does best—use Band-Aids when I need stitches. She wipes my knees to keep me from spilling out. When all I want is to make the gash bigger and bigger and bigger and watch all of me spill over my mother, over my father, until I am everything and nothing. She slaps my hand away because "that's how you get scars"—picking at scabs growing over wounds. She never tells me all the other ways I'll scar. And she'll never slap my hand again, busy with her own scabs. The loops and hooks of my Velcro shoes keep me from falling but at school I'm the wetback, spic baby who can't tie her shoes. And there aren't any ways to explain that my parents did what they could. And we'll never ever feel like enough. And there aren't enough knots, or hooks, or loops to hold me together. I trip, and fall, and gush. I am split skin. Until I learn I am the one who can go through.

Sonia Alejandra Rodríguez is an immigrant of Juarez, Mexico and was raised in Cicero, IL. Her creative writing appears in *Hispanecdotes*, *Every Day Fiction*, *Acentos Review*, *Newtown Literary*, *Longreads*, *Lost Balloon*, *Reflex Fiction*, and elsewhere. She teaches at LaGuardia Community College in New York City. For more information, visit soniaarodriguez.com.

MIRRORS

MICHELLE ROSS

The house I was born in had two mirrors, one in the bathroom and one in the living room. The mirror in the living room was the length of the wall on which it hung. Etched in black on the mirror's surface were mountains and forests of imposing pines. Between the mountains, there was a valley, and in that valley, a lake. When I looked in that mirror, I was imprinted on this landscape.

The mirror in the bathroom was etched with water spots and toothpaste. In that mirror, my face was just my face.

The living-room mirror was lit by the sun, which threw a slab of hard, yellow light onto the carpet below.

The bathroom mirror was lit by four bulbs mounted in a line: bleached skulls. WHAT ALIVE!

The living-room mirror reflected our bookshelves: a set of encyclopedias; a farmer's almanac; a Guinness Book of World Records; faux leather-bound novels with gold-edged pages; two small abstract paintings Dad did before I was born—the colors dark and velvety; a moss-colored vase in which turkey feathers were arranged like flowers.

The bathroom mirror reflected frayed towels draped over the shower rod, a needlepoint Mom had done of a lone palm tree drooping coconuts, the crooked-lid hamper that barely concealed our dirty laundry.

Back then I thought of the living room mirror as belonging to Dad and the bathroom mirror as belonging to Mom. But it was Mom who polished both mirrors each Saturday morning with wadded-up newspaper that stained her hands, while miles away, Dad crept through the tall brush, stalking his prey.

Climax

Michelle Ross is the author of the story collections *There's So Much They Haven't Told You*, winner of the 2016 Moon City Short Fiction Award, and *Shapeshifting*, winner of the 2020 Stillhouse Press Short Fiction Award (and forthcoming in 2021). She is fiction editor of *Atticus Review*.

MED(I)A

C.C. RUSSELL

A story that humanizes the horseman. A story that simply asks questions. A story that politely wonders what the harm is in normalizing a man who wears a mask made from the skin of his dead opponent's face. A story that makes us feel for him, how much work it is to keep this mask moisturized, how it haunts him, shadowing his own eyes this way. A story that shows us that he is no longer himself when he removes the mask. A story that reveals our own fathers to be demons. A story that makes us rethink what we were taught. A story that makes us rethink whether or not we should be taught anything. A story that makes it easier for us to forget. A story that normalizes fear, that crawls in the mud so that we don't have to. A story that makes you feel better, a feel-good tale of the good old boys. A story that tells us all that they accomplished. A story of the monster as a young man. A story that attempts to become a mirror, placing us in the monster's shoes. A story that shows him walking the aisles of the local grocery, sitting forlornly at the counter of the old diner. A story that shows us how his father, too, has hurt him. A story that gives us reasons. A story that asks us what reasons matter. A story that shows that anything that we stand for is made of cardboard in the rain. A story that erases, that builds up something else in its place. A human interest story. A Friday kind of story to take us into the weekend. A story where we find ourselves holding his hand, adjusting his mask lovingly. Look, there are our fingers smoothing his new lips, our soft caress over his beautiful, wrinkled cheek.

C.C. Russell's prose and poetry have been published in such journals as *The Colorado Review*, and *Whiskey Island*. He currently lives in Wyoming with a couple of humans and several cats. You can find more of his work at ccrussell.net

LILLY

SARAH SALWAY

Outside the kitchen window, the daylily grows with every cup of tea you make, exploding from the top of its delicate stalk, cells popping into the early summer air. It's as loud as the helicopter flying low overhead when later you post your library books back one by one, the sound of each hitting the metal floor of the overnight drop box, and the blind man who turns to you, asks if you've ever been to Thailand, he's never had a woman friend before, and as arm in arm you cross the road to his bus stop, he says he listened to a scary story last night and had to sleep with his hands covering his ears so no more words could post themselves back into his head. It's funny, he says, not smiling, then he asks if he can cup your chin, holds it close to his face as if you're the daylily and he can hear you growing.

Sarah Salway is a novelist, teacher and poet from Kent, England. She collects good words and bad jokes, and can be found at www.sarahsalway.co.uk.

FLEAS, MARKETS

PETE SEGALL

The man trades a television for a goat. A woman trades a well-shellacked rocking chair for a sturdy pair of boots. A boy trades his body for a framed picture of a bridge. Some trades are more equitable than others. A very old man with one arm deftly haggles the deed to a distant orchard into two pianos and a cello. One of the pianos is in bad need of tuning but the old man isn't concerned. No trade goes unnoticed. A mother trades her daughter for a sack of fertilizer; the girl trades herself again for a pistol, which she uses to shoot herself through the jaw. There is an argument over who gets possession of the fertilizer. It goes on for days and days. A scrawny, sore-riddled man who came with nothing to trade trades the dead daughter's body for something he is offered in a whisper but negotiates to keep her hipbone and fingers. Patiently he strips off the skin and muscle, which he trades for a bottle of expired antibiotics. Restored to health he plays music by striking the dead daughter's fingerbones against the hip. The music is lovely enough that people are forced to notice. What they hear are their own heartbeats, their own footsteps. The beat of a song in a club, a march, a fervid star's pulse. They hear rage and the moment before rage. They hear birds. They hear vanishing lovers. It is all momentary and piercing, a flash across the unbalanced field of time, fair as theft, kind as theft; accordant, possible.

Pete Segall lives in Chicago.

ZASTRUGI

HIBAH SHABKHEZ

The snow fell in swift soft flakes, and the children rejoiced. When morning came the mountain-slopes would be frozen solid, and they would be allowed to go skiing. The wind had other plans, however. All night it raked and tossed the snow, sculpting it into waves across which the dawn rippled red.

The children raced out into the crimson, but wiser hands pulled them back. "Do not trust the zastrugi," said the elders. "The surface seems steely under the sun, but the still-soft snow lurks underneath, ravening for your blood. Stay inside. Our houses are built strong to withstand the winter's siege."

The snow saw the longing in the children's eyes, and began to squirm under the assaults of the sun, wondering how to prove itself steady enough for the little feet of the children. The eagle of the peak, who had come to scour the farms for cattle or carrion since its natural prey had fallen or flown away, saw this folly and seethed.

The children watched the eagle clawing at the snow, marvelling at the great bird's cruel strength.

161

Out of the clouds with a mighty thrumming came a creature more ferocious yet, a giant white bird spitting flame.

"It was the snow," said the people of the plains afterwards. "The zastrugi buckled, sloughing off the houses and casting them into the river."

"And what did the water do with them?" asked the kin of the people of the mountains.

"Why, what water always does. It bade them welcome."

Hibah Shabkhez is a writer of the half-yo literary tradition, an erratic language-learning enthusiast, and a happily eccentric blogger from Lahore, Pakistan. Studying life, languages and literature from a comparative perspective across linguistic and cultural boundaries holds a particular fascination for her.

THE ANOREXIC'S MOTHER

SHOSHAUNA SHY

Her blue jeans sag. I want to hook on suspenders, hitch them up. I want to hold her, those jutting shoulder blades like a bird with broken wings. I bake cookies so the aroma entices her down from the attic. Spear my 4th helping of brisket. I'm eating for two.

Author of five poetry collections, Shoshauna Shy's flash fiction has appeared in *100 Word Story*, *50-Word Stories*, *Fiction Southeast*, *Sou'wester*, and a multitude of other places. Not a monogamous writer, she usually works on 7-11 different pieces at a time. She is also the founder of PoetryJumpsOff-theShelf.com.

STEEP IT THE COLOUR OF HEDGEROWS AND TWO SUGARS

RACHAEL SMART

This morning the tea man's vending van had been coloured by graffiti. He was hosing and using bronze wool on it and cursing profusely. Never would've happened back in Ireland, he said.

You know, my dad used to keep Ireland in a tin box, I said. Under his bed. I used to peek in at it.

Whereabouts in Ireland was it, though? he said and he jetted water at a capital E.

Can never be too sure, I said, but there were tall blue grasses and the chocolate sounds of a fiddle and my belly reckons Galway. I'll go someday. Hunt down his bloodline. Hold his land. When I can, I said, you know, and I crouched to tie the laces of my runners.

I do know, he said. He put his thumb over the spout of the hose so that the water frisked silver and I thought of the farm my dad was born on, the canter of ponies. Always knew you had the same roots as me, somehow, he said, his slaty eyes stone on me.

Oh yeah, I said, making a church steeple out of my hands, what makes you say that?

Because you're not one to flinch, are you, he said and he turned the surge of water on me. I didn't bolt. Felt the cold blue of it undressing me. I gave him the scythe of a smile, stood firm.

Rachael Smart writes essays, poetry and short fiction. Recent work has been published at *The Letters Page* and *Unthology 11*. Her story *"The Inconsequential Codes on Lipsticks"* was short-listed for The Bristol Short Story Prize 2018.

THE ETERNITY BERRY

GRACE Q. SONG

> *"Don't make me sad, don't make me cry."*
> —Lana Del Rey

Every night has a rhythm until Roo breaks it. One night, after I tuck the blanket under her chin and kiss her forehead, she asks about Mama. She wants to know ten things about her, and I tell her. I tell her about the Beatles records stashed downstairs, the lullaby she used to sing as a sad song. I tell her how much she looks like Mama with her ebony hair and midnight eyes. I tell her how Mama loved blueberries: the hard, the ripe, the sweet, and even the bitter ones. *Like handfuls of love,* she used to say. I tell her how much she loved Baba. How much she hated being his wife. He left for long periods of time, and the neighborhood wives would laugh until she was bone-bruised. I tell Roo about loneliness. *Is that why she's not here anymore?* she asks. Her voice is small. I take her hand and tell her Mama loved her more than all the blueberries in the world. I tell her that sometimes, love just makes people sad. What I don't tell her is how you'll die if you love the wrong person. How Mama loved him until all the blueberries were gone.

Grace Q. Song is a Chinese-American writer residing in New York. Her poetry and fiction have been published or are forthcoming in *Storm Cellar*, *SmokeLong Quarterly*, *Passages North*, *PANK*, *The Journal*, and elsewhere. A high school senior, she will be attending Columbia University in fall 2021.

JUST A FEW FACTS

ANDREW STANCEK

Everyone always wants to remember, every head is full of facts: phone numbers, addresses, birthdays, anniversaries, the date of VE Day and 9/11.

"Remember when," she'd say and of course I always nodded, even if I didn't; no one ever admits not remembering.

I've decided to not remember three new facts a day. Yesterday I surrendered the name of the stuff that comes from cows, the color of the sky and the land mass next to New Zealand. Today it's the taste of lemons, the smell of a camp fire on a fall day and the sound of a flute. I feel lighter already.

The doctor said you are likelier to get hit by lightning twice than to have two such fatalities. I'm sure he means to be helpful, consoling, demonstrating his best bedside manner. I remember our visits to his office and the first ultrasound with the pounding heartbeat. I remember the way Evelyn clutched my hand. I remember our drive to the hospital and the sweat on her forehead, her eardrum-shattering moans and me whisper-screaming, "Breathe,

breathe, breathe."

I remember the nurse's yell, the doctor's snapping, the Code Blue, a white coat taking me by the elbow, "You have to leave the OR now, give the doctors room."

I remember knowing, even before the words came from the doctor's mouth.

Tomorrow I will forget the baby's name, my wife's name, the past month.

Andrew Stancek describes his vocation as dreaming—clutching onto hope, even in turbulent times. He has been published widely, in *SmokeLong Quarterly*, *FRiGG*, *Green Mountains Review*, *New World Writing*, *New Flash Fiction Review*, *Jellyfish Review* and *Peacock Journal*, among others, and he continues to be astonished.

MY CLOSET

SAMANTHA STEINER

My closet has no clothes.

One side: a jewelry chest, a tub of half-used nail polish, a carved Santa presiding over a tree stump.

The other side: a feather quill, a jar of stiff paint brushes, a sewing machine.

The ceiling: a scattering of pale plastic stars.

I close myself inside, and the jewelry chest, the nail polish, the Santa, the quill, the paintbrushes, the sewing machine, and my entire body vanish. Here, I am breath with eyes.

The stars give off a cool light. They appear in the mirrors hidden on the walls, the mirror on the back of the closet door. They glow through nebulae of exhale on glass.

I gaze into my reflection. Little green specks dance under my eyelashes. I stand suspended while billions of miles away, red giants burn.

Samantha Steiner (she / her / hers) is a Fulbright Scholar and visual artist. Her writing has been nominated for *Best of the*

Net and *The Best Small Fictions*. In 2020 she was selected as Featured Fiction Writer by *Lammergeier Magazine* for her story "Pinky Monster." Follow her on Twitter and Instagram @Steiner_Reads.

POSTCARD TOWN

CHELSEA STICKLE

When we were first captured in this postcard, life was as expected. Trash pick-up on Wednesday, recycling on Thursday. Then time began slowing down. A word would last a fraction of a second too long. A raised eyebrow would comically linger. I thought I was just tired, but it kept happening. Soon everyone was huddling and sharing information. It was worse on Main Street, they said. Anywhere scenic. People started staying home. Afraid to get caught under the idyllic blue sky or the sun-dappled trees. Anything that someone might want to see.

Time stretched like taffy. No one went to work anymore. The trash and recycling didn't get picked up. People stopped showering. My arm trailed until it looked like I had several sprouting from the same source. Moving at all became an event. Conversations became impossible. No one could keep track of what had already been said.

It was the golden hour when everything stopped permanently. The sun was setting, and the sky was cotton candy waves of purple, red, and pink. Too beautiful to take a bite out of. But now we're all stuck here, reaching for a glass or cooking chicken, all so you could take a piece of our town, a piece of us with you.

Chelsea Stickle lives in Annapolis, MD with her black rabbit, George and an army of houseplants. Her flash fiction appears in *matchbook*, *Pithead Chapel*, *McSweeney's Internet Tendency* and others. *Breaking Points*, her debut chapbook, is forthcoming from Black Lawrence Press (Fall 2021). Read more at chelseastickle.com/stories and on Twitter @Chelsea_Stickle.

DROSOPHILA MELANOGASTER

HANNAH STORM

The fruit fly shares the same genes as a human. Its Latin name is "Drosophila Melanogaster," which sounds awfully fancy for something attracted to rotten fruit and vegetables. I think about the time you told me I smelt ripe when you forced me onto my back in that room with the torn sheets. Fruit flies breed in drains, empty bottles, and waste disposals, relying on a moist layer of material that ferments to grow their families. The adults have brown trunks, black bottoms, and crimson eyes and are so small they can creep through windows and doors that aren't properly covered. I think about the time we met, how I was bruised and broken, how you flew to my side, hovered around me, your tanned arms winged in a false promise. The reproductive potential of a fruit fly is enormous and given the chance they can lay five hundred eggs. Your first girlfriend had an abortion. You left your second after you boasted how easy it would be for you to get her pregnant. You tell me this as you lie, limp and damp, and I see your eyes turn red with tears. Soon you're snoring. You don't hear me creep away to mop up the smell of me, or move to the window above the bins, where I watch their bags spilling into the car park. Your snores sound like the buzz of five hundred flies surfacing from the fetid food when I leave you in your waste.

Hannah Storm's writing has been published internationally. She's been placed second at the Bath Flash Fiction Award, shortlisted in several awards and made the BIFFY 50. Her debut flash collection is published this year by *Reflex Fiction*. She lives in Yorkshire, England with her husband and two children.

THE CAR TAG KIDS

JENNIFER TODHUNTER

After every funeral, we play car tag. Lift keys from our front hallways, still dressed in black skirts and skinny ties, pair into the driver and passenger seats of our parents' cars, some of us holding memorial handouts, some of us a little drunk from the flask passed around the funeral home bathroom.

We snake curves along the coast, speed away from the gridded roads of our small town, stop at 7-Eleven for slurpees we stud with stolen rum, ask the man collecting change to buy us a pack of Marlboros which we exhale out wide-open windows, the plumes of smoke twinning our exhausts.

We don't talk about the accidents. We listen to mixed CDs stashed underneath our seats instead, hide in invisible shadows of night-lit alleys and wait for someone's headlights to slice the sides of our cars.

Some of us creep through the back streets, our engines a hum above our whispers, our hearts thudding at the possibility of getting spotted. Some of us park and make-out, our bare legs stuttering across leather seats, our hands and feet tangled in dangling belts.

Some of us cry, unsure if loss is ever exhaustive.

And some of us drive—some of us always drive.

We know it's reckless, this addiction to the high-pitched squeal of tires cutting corners. The adrenaline that follows the reverberation of acceleration. The unmistakable sound of locked brakes and the silence that follows. We wait out those deafening seconds with eyes closed, wait until the sound of two vehicles accordioning together comes.

Or doesn't.

And when headlights paint the sides of our cars, when we've been found and tagged, we stomp on our gas pedals, chase brake lights ahead of us until we tap the other car's bumper or lose sight of the ruby red glow around a corner, down a hill, into the invisible distance.

We stay and play until the black blanket of night melts into a dusky indigo. Until our rum-studded slurpees are long gone, our Marlboros stubbed out on the soles of our funeral shoes, and our gas tanks sputter in surrender. We will feed this legacy, we will fight this feeling of euphoria, right down to our last breath, because nobody wants to be it in the morning.

Jennifer Todhunter's stories have appeared in *The Forge*, *River Teeth*, *CHEAP POP*, and elsewhere. Her work has been selected for *The Best Small Fictions*, *Best Microfiction*, and *Wigleaf*'s Top 50 Very Short Fictions. She is the Editor-in-Chief of *Pidgeon-holes* and founder of *Trash Mag*. Find her at www.foxbane.ca or @JenTod_.

AND I STILL REMEMBER HOW YOUR HANDS WERE SO MUCH LARGER THAN MINE

CATHY ULRICH

Outside, it is snowing. The wind makes a sound like a lowing ghost. My brother and his girlfriend dress to go sledding. The girlfriend comes from a place where it never snows. Her skin is sun-dark and she smells like ocean sand. When flakes land on her mouth, she licks them away, swallows them down. She says: *This is beautiful.*

My mother likes this one; my mother liked the last ones too. Series of placid, soft-voiced girls who watch me doing dishes at the sink, who want her recipe for lasagna, who don't eat like this at home, who say *okay* when my brother suggests things like sledding, little hush voices, *okay, okay, okay.*

Outside, it is snowing.

My brother and his girlfriend have found the old childhood sled. It is purpler than I remember. I watch them from the window, write your name into my fog-breathed frost, wipe it away with the back of my suds-wet hand.

My brother and his girlfriend fly down the hill, mouths going open wide, they could be laughing or crying or something else. And they go down and down the hill, and fall away into the white and white and white.

Cathy Ulrich is the founding editor of *Milk Candy Review* and the author of the flash fiction collection *Ghosts of You* (Okay Donkey Press). Her work has appeared in various journals and anthologies. She lives in Montana with her daughter and slightly fewer small animals than they started with.

B IS FOR BALLS

KARA VERNOR

In high school, when a boy threw a ball and another boy caught it, I banged two pom-poms together a few times.

When a boy caught a ball behind the end zone's white line, I banged two pom-poms and kicked a leg. My crotch was wrapped in blue.

There were thirteen of us who bounced and banged.

When the boys gathered on a field mowed for Friday night, the townspeople mobbed the border. These watchers sat on seats called bleachers because boys could throw balls for three hours with the break they took halfway through. When the throwing of balls exhausted the boys, they resorted to their butts like watchers on bleachers, but not we. We stood and shouted and danced and banged for three hours, sometimes more.

On days when boys threw balls, we covered our butts in miniskirts. We recognized the relationship between our nakedness and their confidence, and it was said frostbite was not worse than Nair. While our legs encouraged boys to throw their balls, the townspeople enjoyed the school-sanctioned opportunity to see the whole lengths of our allegiant legs. They appreciated our legs for their service.

School officials otherwise required taller skirts. Short skirts were a violation and declaration unless worn for ball-throwing boys and the townspeople who ran their eyes up our flagpole limbs. It was true, townspeople needed more than strictly boys and the balls that flew between them, but not we. We had never been served by need.

Kara Vernor's fiction and essays have appeared in *Ninth Letter*, *The Normal School*, *Gulf Coast*, *The Best Small Fictions*, and *Wigleaf*'s Top 50. She has received support from the Elizabeth George Foundation and her chapbook, *Because I Wanted to Write You a Pop Song*, is available from Split Lip Press.

THE CHORUS IN MY WALLS

ELISABETH INGRAM WALLACE

Honey I say, honey, I think we have bees, listen I say listen: he freeze frames and listens, and there's an unmistakable thud behind the chipboard; *Badgers?*, he says, *or rats, or a ghost, this is our first house and we have no fucking luck* he says, *of course it's fucking possessed*, No I say, no it's bees, look at the electric socket, and he does, he sees the gold gloop splooging down the eggshell blue, my choice, S*hit* he says, *do you think this will be like France, when we had the millipedes?*, no I say, thinking of how the black walls would scatter scuttle under the floorboards when we flicked on the ampoule to eat le souper Lidl, and the night he'd said "maybe we should have a bit of time apart?", not fucking likely I'd said, and we slept in the car, then I called an exterminator and put it on my credit card and said it was only 200 Euro but I still haven't paid it off, *God I hope not* he says, definitely not, I say, I think it will be more like the time I dropped the crystal champagne glass in the kitchen on our wedding day, and it shattered into a thousand billion splinters, and a full six months on my bare feet will occasionally catch one and bleed profusely, then hurt profusely because crystal cuts they go deep and go black blood hard, and I will not "just put some bloody shoes on" and I will not pull the splinters out either because each time I step-hurt I remember you, that cloudy cold day, the beach the rain the arduously selected Non-Denominational master of ceremonies who turned out to be a religious nut job and rambled about The Judgement Of God for thirty minutes while my mascara ran and you squinted rain and shivered like a puppy and then on the way home my ring disappeared, but I only noticed after an hour after we'd wondered around the town drunk like eejits, and you paced up and down the streets all night looking for it, even up streets we hadn't ever walked down, didn't even know existed, because I was crying and you wanted to make me smile.

Elisabeth Ingram Wallace's work has appeared in *SmokeLong Quarterly*, *Atticus Review* and *Barrelhouse*. Her writing has won a Scottish Book Trust New Writers Award and The Mogford Short Story Prize. In 2020 she won the QuietManDave Prize at Manchester Metropolitan University, and *The Forge Literary Magazine* and *Fractured Lit*'s flash fiction competitions.

NE PLUS ULTRA

NAJAH STEFANY BINT ABDUSH-SHAHID WEBB

The earth was shaking and the picture frames were falling and the car horns were honking and my breath caught and the walls were crumbling and the sun went black and the people screamed and my breath caught and the molten lava poured from the pavement and ran like a river through the streets and rain red like fire came from the sky and my breath caught and they rose from under leaves of grass with all traces of time washed from their flesh like wings broken free from their hard cocoon and my breath caught and my breath caught and my breath caught and my breath caught caught caught when my sweat struck the ground, the room shook once, my breath caught like a volcano erupting into wakefulness as the door to heaven swung open to swallow me in its beautiful warmth.

Najah Webb is the founder of the BIPOC Book Critics Collective. She received recognition from the Hurston Wright Foundation for her microfiction. You can find her longer work in *Kweli Journal* or on Medium. She lives and writes in ATL, GA.

WHEN MOTHER ROASTS A CHICKEN, SHE SHINES

JOYCE ANN WHEATLEY

Bread hot on the table. Chicken in the oven.

These are the best parts, she says, ladling from a pot. Two-fisted, she grips the neck and sucks stewed skin, flesh, fractured bones. Juice greases her chin. I think *nobody else's mother eats like this*. I want bread and butter.

Liver's mashed, gizzard's minced. Last, the heart— shaped like a strawberry. I imagine the muscle thumping within the breast, pumping blood, life. She dices, offers me a morsel. It's chewy and bland.

Golden-brown, the roasted bird rests on a platter. In the pan, she stirs flour into spattering fat, makes a roux, adds all the chopped-up bits, pours in stock, seasons and simmers. Her face shines. She lifts a steaming spoonful to my lips. We both blow. Later, we sop up gravy with the bread. I taste it then, the heart, how it deepens the flavor of everything.

Joyce Ann Wheatley works at the Central Public Library in Ithaca, New York. Her work has appeared in *The A3 Review*, *Gravel Magazine*, *Lost Balloon*, *Stone Canoe*, *Bath Flash Fiction Anthology* and elsewhere.

FAR FROM THIS HOWLING CORNER

CHARMAINE WILKERSON

It took the gazebo, first, the one on the beach where we used to picnic, the one where we'd made our baby on a crickety night. It flipped our neighbors' boats, flattened the school, then came for our roof. It screamed above as we bowed our heads and scrambled for shelter. It smashed the bed where our little girl had slept. It tore up the roads where she'd walked to class. It took places where we'd worked and people we had known. But our daughter was hours away, far from this howling corner. The rest we could handle. Anything else.

Charmaine Wilkerson's microfiction can be found in various magazines and anthologies. Her novella-in-flash *How to Make a Window Snake* won a Bath Novella-in-Flash award and a Saboteur Award for Best Novella. Her debut novel is due for publication in 2022.

TED

EVAN WILLIAMS

Ted wants your birds. They are for his children: Ted's children are worms. They did not start this way. Ted's children drink bird's blood. This is how they became worms.

Ted's family lives in a pile of bread crumbs. He imagines he manages an imaginary menagerie. Ted has never imagined doing anything else. His father manages a more successfully imagined menagerie.

Ted's worms think Ted is a failure. *You are a failure*, they say in unison.

Ted's worms paint their bread crumb pile with bird's blood. The bread crumbs sing a bird song and the worms sing along. Ted does not know the words to the bird song. The worms know the words and everything else Ted does not. Ted does not know he is imaginary. The worms have created him out of branches. Ted is a portal for bird's blood. He cannot exist without your birds.

Ted needs your birds.

Evan Williams is a cornfield who became a student at The University of Chicago. He has work appearing or forthcoming in *HAD*, *Ecotheo*, and *DIAGRAM*, among others.

SAFE HOUSE

SOPHIA WILSON

1

The body opens its doors; an egg is a chamber;
a womb, a home; a home, a refuge; a refuge, safe.

2

A wooden rectangle (thirty by twenty-six centimetres)
slid up and down in a groove, is door to a house.

3

A nearby opening (ten by twelve centimetres) is
doorway to a ramp;

4

A ramp, when trodden on, seesaws as locked door
of a cage.

5

A metal grille (ten by twelve centimetres) at the end
of a cage is also a door, permitting kill, or release.

6

A stoat is (not) enticed (by dried fish, fresh egg, a
dead bird) to climb the ramp (to a trap).

7

Instead, it waits, watching doors that lead to homes.

8

A scattering of leaves, fur and earth, is a door, daily deconstructed and reconstructed by devoted paws.

9

A predator studies a mother's movements in order to study her offspring.

10

Doors are breached; rabbit's kittens, slaughter-scattered; hens, battle-wounded—one down—eggs crushed, yolks gulped. A stoat dances, gloating, teeth bared.

11

A mother feverishly seals nebulous doors—

safety-locks, filters, monitors, limited screen-time.

12

Predators, quintessential, bide time, locate chinks, follow tender scents.

13

A rabbit rebuilds her burrow.

14

A hen rearranges straw in her nesting box.

15

A mother re-secures a hen house; grieves for rabbit doe; re-primes stoat trap; deletes Dealers, Extremists, Haters, Racists, Ruthless Materialists, Pimps and Predatory Cocks from an inbox; gathers her small daughter in, tries to wash her clean.

Sophia Wilson is based in New Zealand. Her poetry / short fiction recently appeared in various journals and anthologies. She has had success in Green Stories and Micro Madness competitions, was runner-up in the 2020 Kathleen Grattan Prize for a Sequence of Poems and winner of the 2020-21 Robert Burns Poetry Competition.

IT'S GHOST TIME AGAIN,

FRANCINE WITTE

and my mother doesn't know. But I know, and it shivers me like stone February to see this ghost that's not at all like my father, who is lonely and clean-shaven. This ghost doesn't give a hoot that my mother is asleep, but I'm not so sure she'd stop it, because if sleeping in separate rooms is any indication, my father hasn't touched her in years. And that started around the time he lost his job and moved himself a sock at a time, a shirt at a time until he was gone. And now they are both sexless, but at least my mother has sleep. Not like it used to be with her walking the floorboards, tango or foxtrot or whatever the hell. I live in the room under hers and when she stopped moving I went up there, and that's when I saw the ghost, his white ghosty sex hand trailing up her nightgown and she'd moan and shift, and she really seemed to like it, big smile crossing her sleepy face, and that's when I came to realize that a ghost can be a better lover than a real-life lover, and it just might change how I think about dating and marriage, which, to tell you the truth is kind of a dead thing anyway.

A FINGERNAIL IS NOTHING

FRANCINE WITTE

until one day it isn't there. Not chipped, not broken. Just a blank space on your fingernub.

Your manicurist wrinkles her nose. Just ignore it, you tell her. Any color is fine.

You weren't hoping for the yellow she finally gives you. You are not one to make a statement or stand out.

Later that night, your back goes flamey with hives. You've been meaning to get to what's causing them. Potato chips, maybe. Or maybe, your lover, Hank.

Your lover, Hank, has been showing up less and less. Your mouth tells him you understand whenever he finally calls.

You fall asleep, potato chip crumbs on your chest. You were testing to see if they were the cause, and they aren't. Your hives are gone and also two more fingernails.

You think about calling Hank. Really make him listen. Tell him that your heart is a flower that needs to be watered.

You return to the nail salon. Would Hank even

listen to you with naked fingers? You can always buy a backscratcher, you tell yourself. And you tell the manicurist, the one who wrinkled her nose, that you want all of your fingers painted bright screaming scarlet.

When she says she can't polish fingernails that she can't see, you tell her that it would be a good thing for her to learn to see what isn't there.

Francine Witte's poetry and fiction have appeared in *Smokelong Quarterly*, *Wigleaf*, *Mid-American Review*, *Passages North*, and many others. Her latest books are *Dressed All Wrong for This* (Blue Light Press,) *The Way of the Wind* (Ad Hoc Fiction,) and *The Theory of Flesh*. She lives in NYC.

REJECTED ENDINGS
FOR *TITANIC*

R. P. WOOD

In one of them, Jack sinks beneath the waves, but he meets a mermaid. The mermaid kisses him and the kiss means he can breathe underwater. The mermaid's hair and Jack's hair billows around their heads like halos, and they end up living in one of the *Titanic*'s fancy staterooms after cleaning all the bodies out.

In another, Jack is perfectly preserved in ice, and floats around the Atlantic for almost a century before scientists discover him and thaw him out. He regains the use of his limbs and facial muscles, and goes to adult drama classes. Later he stars in a movie about his life under an Italian pseudonym, which gives him an exotic flavour.

Alternatively, Rose doesn't throw the necklace into the ocean, but sells it, presumably for a large sum of money. She then invests in Amazon and founds a charity called Like a French Girl, which helps connect underprivileged teenage girls with handsome, floppy-haired boys who then draw their portraits. Afterwards there is always a tour of the vintage automobile museum.

In the last one, the ship doesn't even hit the iceberg. Rose goes on to marry Billy Zane and have three children, before succumbing to the Spanish flu. Jack lives on the streets of New York City for a few years as a bum, surviving a bout of tuberculosis. In 1917 he is drafted into the US Army, and is eventually shot to death at Cantigny on the Western Front. His body is never found.

R. P. Wood is a writer from Tauranga, New Zealand.

OTHER PEOPLE

BENJAMIN WOODARD

Early April. Buds on trees. School and work canceled for the foreseeable future. Nobody leaving the house except for emergencies. My young daughter is bored, I miss my mistress, and my wife can barely stand looking at the two of us. To keep the peace, I arrange two full days of daddy-daughter time in the basement. We saw and hammer. Measure twice. Cut once. Sawdust covers our clothes. The floor. I convince myself I am a good father. The project, I tell my wife, is a dollhouse. And by the second evening, we do produce a two-room abode. And, yes, once we have all the sanded pieces together, colored the rooms in marker and paint, arranged the plastic furniture, I carry the structure to my daughter's room and say, "Fill it with imagination." But beyond pleasing my daughter, beyond distracting her and giving my wife a breather, I use the dollhouse project to quell my own frustrations and loneliness, for the two rooms my daughter and I build are miniature elements of my mistress's apartment, reconstructed from memory. There's the living room, where we sometimes watch television. The bedroom, where we roll around and I feel young. My daughter's toys are more Goodwill than Pottery Barn, so the furniture isn't completely correct. But the placement is as exact as I can remember. The walls the right colors, or at least the colors I think feel right. I even add a mark on the floor. An inside joke. The time we knocked a candle onto the carpet. Singed the fiber. And after my wife and I put our daughter to bed, after we read her a story and she drifts off, I lie to my wife. Say I want to watch our girl sleep. Say it brings me comfort in these confusing times. My wife doesn't care. Anyway, she likes having the whole bed to herself. So I stay in my daughter's room and crawl to the dollhouse. Place my hand inside the small rooms. Concentrate. Imagine. Replay memories. I text my lover a photo. I wait for a response. Her across town, locked inside. Me, illuminated by a Doc McStuffins nightlight, locked inside. In this way, I can't feel her. But maybe she can feel me trying from afar. Feel me not forgetting about the life we'll never share.

Benjamin Woodard is Editor-in-Chief at *Atlas and Alice Literary Magazine*. He lives in Connecticut with his wife and teaches English. This is his second appearance in *Best Microfiction*. Find him online at benjaminjwoodard.com.

MOON PILLOW

JENNIFER WORTMAN

After three days, my husband comes home with the moon pillow, still in its plastic. I don't know how he paid for it. Maybe he didn't.

"For you," he says. Nothing else. He's stopped explaining his disappearances and I've stopped asking. I already know more than I want.

My current pillow is so old it's turned yellow like a book page and almost as flat. The last time my husband vanished, he brought me pajamas that feel like summer on my skin. He always knows what to bring me.

"Why's it a moon pillow?" I ask.

"Because there's moondust inside."

How is that even possible? I don't say. I also don't say, I thought you were dead. I always think he's dead. It doesn't matter what I think.

I pull the moon pillow from the plastic. It's attractively puffy, the opposite of my husband's deflating face. I strip my old pillow, stuff the moon pillow in the case. Like magic, the pillow shrinks to fit its confines, then expands them.

I expect something special when I lay down my head, but it's just a pillow, propping my neck too high. I miss my gross flat cushion. But then the back of my head gets a twinkling feeling that spreads. Pretty soon I'm outer space, dark and sparkling, my edges unseen.

"What do you think?" my husband asks.

I don't want my words to knock the good feeling loose.

"That good, huh?" he says. He knows me so well. Like in the bible. To know someone is to live inside them and also absorb them so they live inside you.

My husband lies down beside me and disappears again, in a different way. The sides of his face are cool, dry caves. His eyes, tunnels. No ring on his twig finger: it fell off or he sold it.

Still, he's enormous. I can't find the end of him.

I scoot over, share my darkness, every speck.

I throw him the moon.

Jennifer Wortman is a National Endowment for the Arts fellow and the author of the story collection *This. This. This. Is. Love. Love. Love.* She lives with her family in Colorado.

CODE BABY

LUCY ZHANG

I initialized constants for your name, variables for your height and weight, buffer sizes for your capacity to learn. The code appeared in a spew of semicolons and letters, incrementing and transferring and accessing memory segments that you'd grow into. You'd find solace in an aluminum box, operating between 5% and 90% noncondensing humidity, a Beryllium-free environment. You'd age, become more complex, a pile of hacks and one-off conditionals—security by obfuscation—and the occasional glitch.

Uncaught exception: object cannot be nil
    You were there and then you weren't: an empty
        crib, lollipop-patterned sheets flat, untouched

Some cryptographic state information was unavailable
    The secrets whispered by your fetal heartbeat,
        I could never hear

Error: use of undeclared identifier
    I saw something the compiler did not, an
        unhackable placenta

Malloc: error for object ADDRESS: double free
Killed you once, removed you twice, uterus
sucked clean, spirits swept into graves

You stopped growing in megabytes. You crashed, panicked, spun up the CPU until my skin burned. UML diagrams, flow-charts, object-oriented design—I planned. I swear I planned. I implemented and built this thing to last. Like a bird, I laid an egg, expelled from my body as a yolk missing its shell. I couldn't get it to work again, couldn't glue it back together with bit flips and binary, so I buried it in a hole.

Lucy Zhang writes, codes, and watches anime. She reads for *Barren Magazine*, *Heavy Feather Review* and *Pithead Chapel*. Find her at https://kowaretasekai.wordpress.com/ or on Twitter @Dango_Ramen.

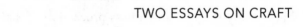

TWO ESSAYS ON CRAFT

Our staff editors asked Avra Margariti, with 2 included stories in Best Microfiction 2021, to talk about her process.

SMALL APOCALYPSES

AVRA MARGARITI

When I write short fiction, I like to keep in mind the following quote by Neil Gaiman: "There's no big apocalypse. Just an endless procession of little ones." This is especially true of microfiction. My personal interpretation is that the world doesn't stop for us, no matter how we might wish it would, if only to mirror our inner pain. It keeps spinning while the people who populate it deal with their own little ends of the world. What might be insignificant in the grand scheme of the cosmos, is so very important to our own selves and loved ones.

This is my approach to flash and microfiction. Events great and terrible could be unfolding in the world over the story's timeline. Although those events inform the protagonist's struggles, they are also a backdrop that complements or contradicts the inner workings of the protagonist's life.

But that's not to say the "small apocalypse" model is egocentric. It stretches to encompass other people and communities; I like to believe solidarity exists even when our world is ending. Ultimately, on top of perspective, it's also a matter of scale—macro- for the world, meso- for community, and micro- for the self. If I ever gather all my short-shorts into a single collection, I will probably name it "Just Another Small Apocalypse."

In "A Dog Like a Ghost," one of my two winning stories, the main character deals with forces both outside and within the self. They grapple with mental illness, and with the way the health system has failed them. My protagonist also shares a living space with a number of house guests / house ghosts. Whether the rest of the world faces a ghost outbreak is left to the readers' interpretation. This vagueness is deliberate, inspired by many works of magical realism, in which strange events often occur within small communities, families, or even spaces of single occupants, without being clear whether the phenomena are universal. The protagonist tries to care for their spectral housemates, and ensure the ghosts enjoy the autonomy they themselves were denied in the past. After the dog's spontaneous adoption, the main character faces another little Armageddon: the overwhelming anger they feel toward those responsible for the dog's injuries.

The focal point of "A Dog Like a Ghost" is spectres

of all kinds contained within the four walls of a haunted house: sad ghosts, a rescue dog, and the protagonist who sees themself in both; all trying to heal and break free.

Prompt From "A Dog Like a Ghost"

Write a story in which one or more animals are present. The animals may serve an allegorical purpose; however, they must be intrinsic to the plot.

Our staff editors asked Jeff Friedman, with 2 included stories in Best Microfiction 2021, to talk about his process.

CRAFT ESSAY AND WRITING PROMPT

JEFF FRIEDMAN

Several months ago while on the telephone with my sister, she began recounting the tragedies that befell her in childhood. There was quite a list, but one stood out to me. She said that my other sister had picked up the piano and heaved it at her, knocking her across the living room of our very small apartment and injuring her arm. "That's why I didn't pursue a career as a classical pianist," she said. I didn't see how my other sister who struggled to carry her stack of books to school could heave a piano, but determination can move mountains.

I told my eldest sister that I didn't remember this incident, but I did remember how in our childhood she had mysteriously started bleeding from every pore in her body. "We had to store you in the bathtub so you would drain into the tub." I recounted for her how mother and I collected her blood in pitchers and then she would drink it back down while our other sister practiced on the out-of-tune piano with the broken legs. Fortunately, a doctor from Barnes Hospital came up with a miracle cure. He taped her like a mummy until she stopped bleeding. She didn't remember, even though it had gone on for three years.

I then told her about how I had double pneumonia in second grade and was out of school for seven plus months, and our mother was worried that the teacher would get the idea that I was just at home doing nothing but reading comics and watching TV, so she invited everyone over to the house and baked desserts and insisted that I recite the names of all the presidents. As I recited their names, the other students slipped out one by one, so by the time I got to Truman, I was talking only to my teacher, who applauded politely. When I got to the kitchen, they had polished off all the baked goods and vanished. When I came back to school, they had a new joke: "Friedman's room is so small he sleeps standing up." My sister said that she didn't remember that I had double pneumonia, not even the contraption with the hoses and the suction cups on the faucet in the bathroom.

Several weeks later, my sister began remembering bad things that happened to her in the past. "When I was in second grade," she said, "I had double pneumonia. I missed almost all of my elementary school years." Then she told me that Mother had baked for the kids in her class, and she had performed malaguena. "Wait a minute," I said, "You didn't have double pneumonia; I had it." We argued for a good hour about who had double pneumonia. "I had it too," she said. Then I remembered we didn't actually have a piano. She remembered that I wasn't her brother. I remembered that neither of us had another sister. "No more calls," we both shouted at the same time. Thus I lost a sister, but gained a new story, "Lost Memory."

Prompt from "Lost Memory"

> *Write a microstory in which one character steals something very unusual—even something that might seem impossible to steal—from another character.*

WHAT THE EDITORS SAY: INTERVIEWS WITH THE YEAR'S TOP MICROFICTION MAGAZINES

INTERVIEW WITH MICHELLE ELVY BY KATHRYN KULPA

FLASH FRONTIER: AN ADVENTURE IN SHORT FICTION

Four stories from Flash Frontier *were chosen for* Best Microfiction 2021. *That's impressive! As a journal that specializes in microfiction, do you see the form as essentially flash fiction with a shorter word count, or do you have different standards for micros?*

Thank you! We are thrilled, especially as we've seen how the form has taken hold over the last ten years in Aotearoa, New Zealand, where *Flash Frontier* is based. Three of the four writers whose work was selected for inclusion are from New Zealand. Others are relatively new to writing micros—which is exciting to see.

Word count is obviously the first thing that makes a micro a micro, but it's more than that.

A piece that is 250 words—the main focus of *Flash Frontier* inclusions—has to work even harder than a piece twice the length or the much "larger" flash of 1,000 words. It's not merely a story truncated; there's a particular focus needed. It's a delight to see when a writer gets the angle just right. That's not to say there is only one "just right"—the micro, with its tighter word count restriction, encourages even more experimentation. A micro has to use the space with tremendous economy, which means it must also pay particular attention to style. I think with a micro you find writers taking the challenge even further, in terms of content *and form*. The exploration can go both wide and deep. The options for creativity are limitless.

Following up on the previous question: what makes a microfiction piece stand out for you? Language? Story? Character? Something else?

We find the best micros are language-driven, sometimes even carefully working that line between prose and poetry. We love how a small, focused scene may be more about the essential mood than anything else. The way it implies a hard-to-put-to-words feeling. Sometimes a small turn of phrase can be nearly perfect. That really stands out in a micro. If it is about character, it's usually something around a new view, an unexpected moment, experience or even collision. A micro, even if about character with a clear narrative arc, is never static—there is a kinetic energy that is a critical element.

I've noticed that Flash Frontier *publishes quarterly themed issues, and that you also use guest editors. Can you talk about how that works: how you choose themes, how much leeway writers have in interpreting those themes, and how the magazine has evolved over time through different guest editors: what has changed, what's still the same?*

We started in 2012 with monthly issues, but we moved to quarterly a couple years later. The issues are always themed. We like themes to be widely, and *wildly*, interpreted. Works included can be directly or obliquely related to the topic. Our very first issue, setting up our urge to explore the form, was "Frontiers". Last year, we saw diverse interpretations of "water", "machines", "Matariki" (the Māori name for Pleiades) and "doors". In 2019, we explored genres, from romance to comedy to historical fiction. In 2018 we took a trip around the world, from Africa to Antarctica to the Pacific. This year, we have both "sweet" and "sour" in the mix. We hope the themes we choose allow exploration of structure and content.

Our philosophy around guest editors is that they help expand the scope of contents. It also keeps us on our toes—we learn something new each time we work with other editors, as we move through their selections and edits. Each editor reads with a different lens. Often, the guest editors will have expertise around the theme or idea: Pia Z. Ehrhardt and Paula Morris edited the "New Orleans" issue; John O Ndavula edited "Africa"; and A J Fitzwater and Tim Jones edited "speculative fiction". We brought in Tania Hershman and Kathy Fish for "science", and Tino Prinzi for "comedy". We try to invite people from diverse writing backgrounds to guest edit, from David Gaffney to Christopher Allen to Apirana Taylor.

I know you publish a special issue featuring stories from National Flash Fiction Day. Can you tell us a little bit about National Flash Fiction Day in New Zealand and your connection with it?

National Flash Fiction Day was founded in New Zealand in 2012, the same year as the journal. We had just wrapped the *52|250 – A Year of Flash* project, and I wanted to focus more locally, in New Zealand where I lived. I collaborated with Kerikeri writing friend Sian Williams. There was no journal for flash in NZ, but as we started to explore, we discovered that there were plenty of precursors, including an anthology edited by Graeme Lay, *100 New Zealand Short Short Stories* (1997). We asked Graeme to collaborate, and he agreed to judge the first competition, with Tina Shaw and Stephen Stratford. It was Graeme who came up with the idea of hosting NFFD on the shortest day of the year which, in the southern hemisphere, is June 22. From the 2012 competition—which was surprisingly popular—NFFD took off. Now the annual celebration sees the national competition, an international youth competition and six coordinated events, from the far north to the deep south. 2020 was a bit different as we were all in COVID lockdown, and NFFD was bit hybrid and online—but all the more robust because of it.

Let's say a writer wants to submit to Flash Frontier. Are there one or two pieces you would recommend they read to get a good sense of your aesthetic?

A very hard question to answer! Quite often, writers surprise us—and we like to encourage an expansive approach to the form, rather than trying to apply too many parameters around style or aesthetics. We also tend to encourage new writers—and work directly, and sometimes rigorously, with writers around edits. If there is a kernel of something there, a small thing that may be teased out with a bit more of a push, we'll take it on. It's a learning experience all around. Which may inform some of our aesthetics, alongside a standard for strong writing.

Perhaps the best examples might be the ones that were selected by *Best Microfiction* this year, as each one demonstrates something different, from the exploratory feel of Patrick Pink's "The Book of What If" to the experimental form of Sophia Wilson's "Safe House", from the dark comedy of R. P. Wood's "Rejected Endings for *Titanic*" to the haunting imagery of Hibah Shabkhez's "Zastrugi".

It's worth noting, too, that the editing team reflects

our diverse interests and experience. James Norcliffe, Vaughan Rapatahana and Gail Ingram are poets first and foremost, with vast experience between them in other forms too (James is also an award-winning children's author). Sam Averis and Rachel Smith are experienced writers of small fictions, although Rachel is expanding into novel-writing and Sam's creative curiosity roams far and wide. Meanwhile, guest editors include poets, playwrights, memoirists, historical fiction novelists, romance writers and more. Perhaps this, too, reflects our arms-wide-open approach to our project.

INTERVIEW WITH SCOTT GARSON BY PAT FORAN

WIGLEAF

Congratulations on having three Wigleaf *pieces selected for* Best Microfiction 2021. *How have you seen the (very) short fiction form change or grow since you began publishing it in 2008?*

Thank you!

When I really put myself back there, in *Wigleaf*'s birth year, it seems like the biggest change has to do with the writers. There weren't as many journals publishing flash in '08, and there weren't as many people writing it. Now, it's like nearly every young writer tries their hand at very short fiction, and this infusion—of diverse talents and perspectives and voices—has done wonders for the form. People can't ignore flash fiction anymore (see, for example, *The New Yorker*, which has started publishing it).

How has Wigleaf *changed and / or grown over that same span? How would you characterize the* Wigleaf *aesthetic? Has it evolved, as well?*

As an editor, I was very comfortable running *Wigleaf* in its upstart years, before we started getting Pushcarts. I had a couple of goals, which I wouldn't have acknowledged, and which I might not have even recognized for what they were. But I had them: I wanted to publish first-rate stuff, like as good as you could read anywhere, print or otherwise. And I wanted that first-rate stuff to be different from other first-rate stuff. Different from *Ploughshares* and *Tin House*, and even *Conjunctions*. That's to say that I probably saw the *Wigleaf* aesthetic as a counter-aesthetic. As we've matured and gained status (taking on staff and formalizing editorial processes, all that), we've had to ask interesting questions about what we want to do, aesthetic-wise. Because *so* much good writing comes our way these days. I'd say we're still eager to be surprised, though. I hope that's a permanent characteristic.

> *More congratulations are in order—your own story "Junk" (published in* Bluestem Magazine*) was selected for* Best Microfiction 2021. *What excites you, the writer, about the micro form?*

Thank you! I love writing micros, in part because it's not work. I don't mean that I don't work on them. I do. I'm a good American. Hard work, grindstone, etc. I mean writing micros doesn't take that much commitment or discipline. The way I do them, conception and composition happen nearly simultaneously, so I'm seeing what I've got. I'm following myself. I'll edit and rewrite later, maybe. Or trash them. Either way.

I had this process streamlined during the time when I did "Junk." I was writing a whole lot of micros, all of one paragraph, all on my phone. I've got the best ones in a manuscript now, *Stories of No Real Use.*

In a 2008 interview with The Elegant Variation, *you referred to (very) short fiction as "something still new, something still being wandered, explored." Is it still new, still being wandered, still being explored? If so, what is it about the form that keeps it fresh and frontier-ish?*

I like what that Scott Garson guy had to say in *The Elegant Variation.* That's not bad.

And I do think very short fiction is still frontier-ish. Writers are definitely out there, seeing what can be done. How different is this from the short story genre, or even the novel? I don't know. One difference: In the case of both the novel and the full-length short story, you have a lot of authorities out there delivering wisdom to would-be practitioners. *If you want to write a good short story, you need to have A and B and C, and you need to do X and Y and Z.* And whatever they say, it's always bullshit, of course. And everyone can see that. None of the people who are actually writing great short stories have A and B and C and do X and Y and Z. So I don't know. But just the fact that very short fiction is authority-less, for the most part—that's good. It's good.

> *The* Wigleaf *postcards that accompany the (very) short fiction you publish are fabulous. They comprise a micro venue all its own. Any plans to issue them as a set, suitable for mailing? Absent that—what's next (or could be next) for the dimensional plane called* Wigleaf?

A set suitable for mailing! How great would that be.

If I say, *We're keeping our options open*, I couldn't fault you for inferring, *They've got no plan*. And it's true: We plan as we go. I'd encourage you to see that as appropriate, for a mag of our ostensible nature.

INTERVIEW WITH ERIC ANDREW NEWMAN BY PAT FORAN

OKAY DONKEY

Five micros first published in Okay Donkey *are in* Best Microfiction 2021—*congratulations! Each of the five stories has its own funny / sad, not-of-this-world-so-much-as-in-it quality, and maybe the only thing they have in common is they're voice driven. When you're reading, what one thing— whether it's something you see, hear, or feel—has to be there in the work if you're going to publish it?*

Well, I think you hit the nail on the head in the question. With micros, there's not a lot of room to write complicated plots or drawn-out character development. The best tool in your toolbox is how to say what you want to say, how to make it sound fresh, unique, and original. And you can do that in large part with a distinctive voice.

For example, four out of the five *OKD* pieces that were accepted this year are in first person. Getting to hear the main character speak in their own voice goes a long way in getting the reader to sympathize with the main character's plight, no matter how outlandish, in a very short period of time. In

Lauren Friedlander's "Alice in Voreland," the main character has such an unusual way of speaking and using of syntax that it drew me in immediately.

How has short fiction evolved—from the stories you read in your queue or the stories you read in the world outside the OKD realm—since you set up shop in May 2018?

Hmmm. Since it's only been a few years since we began—it's kind of tricky to say. I think a lot of these kinds of evolutions can take up to five or 10 years to fully track. You do mention "hermit crab" flash down below, and one thing I have noticed recently is that more and more short short stories are being told in really innovative forms and styles.

While not a "hermit crab" per se, one thing I loved about Elisabeth Ingram Wallace's "The Chorus in My Walls" is that it's written in a single, long, breathless sentence. It's like the reader is tapped straight into the main character's stream of consciousness, so we're tumbling along from image to image, and back and forth in time according to what the character finds the most interesting at that exact second.

Reading, writing, publishing and pushing the parameters of short fiction during a pandemic: What, if anything, felt like it changed, or was beginning to change—again, in your queue, or in the world around you, in your own writing (if you're willing to share)—during COVID-colored 2020? How is it manifesting itself in the work?

Since the last four years were already a pretty dark and bleak time, even before COVID, I noticed that a major shift in my own writing actually happened prior to the pandemic. A lot of my fiction from 2017 and before, had a fairly dark, realistic tone. Once the world itself became so dark and bleak in 2017, I noticed that my stories had become lighter, funnier, and more absurd.

I also think this has found its way into the work we select to publish, as well. I think Kara Vernor's "B is for Balls" is a good example of this in that it's about serious issues like American sexism and the objectification of young women, but it's also written in a sharp, funny, biting style that at times can be really entertaining.

We're seeing more dimensional use of the form(s)—e.g., multimedia and hypertext work, so-called "hermit crab" stuff, and work that is otherwise unclassifiable (in the best best best of ways). What excites you about the current state of short fiction (define "current" and "state" and "short fiction" any way you like)? What excites you about where short fiction might be heading?

As mentioned above, I do really like "hermit crab" flash and short short stories written in all kinds of different forms and styles. One of my favorite micros we've ever published was Kim Magowan's "Madlib," in the form, of course, of a mad lib. There have also been really great recent stories in the form of a crossword puzzle like K.B. Carle's "Vagabond Mannequin" from *Jellyfish Review*, a Venn diagram like Marisa Crane's "When the Light Betrays Us Twice" from *Cotton Xenomorph*, and instructions for a bar of soap like Jennifer Fliss's "All in One Magic Soap" from *Barren Magazine*.

I think with short fiction, you're really only limited in what you can do by your own ideas. You touched on the hyperconnectivity of the world today above and I really love how much Darren Nuzzo's "Stranger Disconnected" uses the Internet, chatrooms, and message boards to tell such a strange little story of how people can connect so deeply online over such long distances, simply by changing a single letter.

Okay Donkey *began as an online lit mag publishing flash and poetry. A year later, you entered the print world with OKD Books. What's next for* Okay Donkey?

We've just been discussing that very thing the last few weeks! Since we have grown so much in the last year, the thing we're working on the most right now is stabilizing and figuring out how to stay that way. We started out as a very small lit mag and over the past year and a half have expanded exponentially.

As a result, we're going to need to expand our staff to keep up.

We started out as just two people in a tiny one-bedroom apartment and now we have four staff on the mag side. We're thinking we should probably at least double that, since the number of submissions we get have easily doubled, if not tripled over just the past year. We're also tinkering around a bit with how to streamline our workflow, but not anything that our wonderful fans and customers will be able to notice.

BEST MICROFICTION THANKS THE JOURNALS WHERE THESE PIECES APPEARED IN 2020.

ALL MATERIAL USED BY PERMISSION.

"Ne Plus Ultra" by Najah Webb from *805 Lit + Art*.

"Instructions for Cleaning A Mirror" by Sarah Freligh and "Far From this Howling" by Charmaine Wilkerson from *100 Word Story*.

"When Mother Roasts a Chicken, She Shines" by Joyce Ann Wheatley from *A3 Review*.

"Myth Bitch" by Noʻu Revilla from *Anomaly*.

"It Finally Happened" by Jad Josey and "Tonight" by Hema Nataraju from *Atlas and Alice Literary Magazine*.

"A World Beyond Cardboard" by Jonathan Cardew, "The Ringmaster's Boys" by Frankie McMillan, and "A Fingernail is Nothing" by Francine Witte from *Atticus Review*.

"City of Serena" by Dawn Raffel from *Big Other*.

"The Anorexic's Mother" by Shoshauna Shy from *Blink Ink*.

"Junk" by Scott Garson from *Bluestem Magazine*.

"Just a Few Facts" by Andrew Stancek from *Boston*

Literary Magazine.

"Postcard Town" by Chelsea Stickle from *Cease, Cows.*

"The Eternity Berry" by Grace Q. Song from *CHEAP POP.*

"Some Meaning—" by Leonora Desar from *Cincinnati Review.*

"Hemiboreal" by Elsa Nekola from *Cincinnati Review* (forthcoming from *Willow Springs Books*).

"My Closet" by Samantha Steiner from *Citron Review.*

"It's Ghost Time Again" by Francine Witte from *Cleaver Magazine.*

"Forest Elegy" by Despy Boutris from *Craft.*

"lilac bed" by Tarah Knaresboro from *Electric Literature.*

"Streets" by Xoşman Qado from *Epiphany.*

"What I'm Made Of" by Ruth Joffre from *Fiction Southeast.*

"a list of things that are white" by Matt Kendrick from *Fictive Dream.*

"The Book of What If" by Patrick Pink, "Zastrugi" by Hibah Shabkhez, "Safe House" by Sophia Wilson, and "Rejected Endings for Titanic" by R.P. Wood from *Flash Frontier: An Adventure in Short Fiction.*

"Windows" by Ranjabali Chaudhuri, "Beating the Herring" by Marie Gethins, and "Foundering" by

Matthew Richardson from *FlashBack Fiction*.

"Magic Bullet" by Bill Merklee and "Moon Watching" by Regan Puckett from *FlashFlood*.

"Ghoul" by Noa Covo, "Of Photography and Truth" by Jason Jackson, and "Moon Pillow" by Jennifer Wortman from *Fractured Lit*.

"In the Aftermath of Hurricane Maria" by Christopher Gonzalez, "Ted" by Evan Williams, and "Other People" by Benjamin Woodard from *HAD*.

"The Car Tag Kids" by Jennifer Todhunter from *Hobart Pulp*.

"Three Postcards" by Kathleen McGookey from *Ilanot Review*.

"Asymmetry" by K-Ming Chang from *Jellyfish Review*.

"The Glowing" by Tara Lindis from *Kenyon Review Online*.

"Something Like Happy" by Emily Devane, "Rehearsal" by Nuala O'Connor, and "Velcro Shoes" by Sonia Alejandra Rodríguez from *Lost Balloon*.

"Steep It the Colour of Hedgerows and Two Sugars" by Rachael Smart from *Lunate*.

"Sisters" by Cezarija Abartis, "Cactus" by Di Jayawickrema, "Red" by Melissa Ostrom, and "Lilly" by Sarah Salway from *Matchbook Literary Magazine*.

"Roadrunners" by Kathryn Kulpa, "The Clown King" by Avra Margariti, and "an essay about ghosts" by Lee Patterson from *Milk Candy Review*.

"Places I Have Peed" by Epiphany Ferrell from *Miracle Monocle*.

"Fairy Tale in Which You Date the Morally Ambiguous Boy in Math" by Charlotte Hughes from *Monkeybicycle*.

"Arrhythmia" by Shareen K. Murayama from *MORIA Literary Magazine*.

"I've Seen Bigger" by Lori Sambol Brody from *New Flash Fiction Review*.

"Lost Memory" by Jeff Friedman, "Not Everything Was in My Father's Will" by Jeff Friedman, and "Mirrors" by Michelle Ross from *New World Writing*.

"A Short List Explaining Why I'm An Okay Person" by Kat L'Esperance-Stokes from *Newfound*.

"It's 5am-ish and my father tells me a story from his time in Singapore" by Exodus Oktavia Brownlow and "Matt's Basement" by Leonora Desar from *No Contact*.

"Alice in Voreland" by Lauren Friedlander, "Stranger Disconnected" by Darren Nuzzo, "There's a Trick With a Knife" by Meghan Phillips, "B is for Balls" by Kara Vernor, and "The Chorus in My Walls" by Elisabeth Ingram Wallace from *Okay Donkey*.

"Eternal Night at the Nature Museum, a Half-hour Downriver from Three Mile Island" by Tyler Barton from *Passages North*.

"Rapunzel, let down your" by Faye Brinsmead and "On Hesitation" by Taylor Byas from *perhappened mag*.

"The Dinosaurs that Didn't Die" by Sarah Bates and "A Girl Opens a Museum" by Ruth Joffre from *Pidgeonholes*.

"There are Frijoles Pintos Lost Inside the Sofa" by Moisés R. Delgado from *Puerto Del Sol*.

"Armadillo Jesus" by Carson Markland from *Smokelong Quarterly*.

"Ornithologia Corvidae" by Sarah McPherson from *Splonk*.

"Autopsy Report" by Abigail Oswald and "med(I) a" by C.C. Russell from *takahē magazine*.

"Fleas, Markets" by Pete Segall from *The Adroit Journal*.

"A Dog Like a Ghost" by Avra Margariti from *The Baltimore Review*.

"P h i l t r u m" by Sudha Balagopal from *The Dribble Drabble Review*.

"When Alice Became the Rabbit" by Cyndi MacMillan from *The Ekphrastic Review*.

"Stella Is" by Claire Polders from *The Mambo Academy of Kitty Wang*.

"Half Moon Bay" by K-Ming Chang from *The Offing*.

"Shut Your Mouth and Listen" by Roberta Beary and "Some Roses Only Need Pepsi" by Angela Readman from *The Phare*.

"Burials" by Despy Boutris from *The Roadrunner Review*.

"Code Baby" by Lucy Zhang from *Third Point Press*.

"Parade" by Garrett Biggs from *Threadcount*.

"What The Dreaming Town Says To You, You in This *Only* Love" by Pat Foran from *Tiny Molecules*.

"When We Were Young" by Christopher M. Drew and "A Desert Graveyard" by Minyoung Lee from *Trampset*.

"Floaters" by Anne Cooperstone from *Variety Pack*.

"Finale" by Christopher Linforth and "And I Still Remember How Your Hands Were So Much Larger Than Mine" by Cathy Ulrich from *Whale Road Review*.

"She's Gone" by Frances Gapper, "Neighbors" by Erinrose Mager, and "Good Stretch" by Rebecca Meacham from *Wigleaf*.

"Drosophila Melanogaster" by Hannah Storm (forthcoming from *Reflex Fiction*) and "The Correct Hanging of Game Birds" by Rosie Garland from *X-R-A-Y Literary Magazine*.

CPSIA information can be obtained
at www.ICGtesting.com
Printed in the USA
LVHW030157070821
694637LV00007B/1183